Fetters
of a
Mind-Set

We Travel on a Journey through the Seasons
With Daniel Steppe as he
Unravels the Enigma of 'The Bible' and the 'Word of God'
And

Who Are You?
The Walk of a Christian Disciple.
The Love of Jesus Christ.

Caroline Webb

BALBOA PRESS

A DIVISION OF HAY HOUSE

Balboa Press books may be ordered through booksellers or by contacting:

Balboa Press
A Division of Hay House
1663 Liberty Drive
Bloomington, IN 47403
www.balboapress.com
1 (877) 407-4847

Print information available on the last page.

ISBN: 978-1-4525-2784-0 (sc)
ISBN: 978-1-4525-2785-7 (e)

Balboa Press rev. date: 03/05/2015

FOREWORD

"Fetters of A Mind Set" is a cleverly written tale based on a fictitious character by the name of Daniel. Daniel is a lad of a common make up, but discovers the word of God as contained in the Holy Bible. His struggle to find where he belongs in the world leads him to divine guidance gained through his readings of the Holy Scriptures.

The story of Daniel is total fiction, but the entire book is scarcely fiction as there is contained within these pages a great number of Biblical quotations and references. This story demonstrates the struggle that many have in growing up, in what can well be described as a confusing environment. Peer pressure draws folk particularly young folk in directions they may well be uncomfortable with. Val Taylor has used Daniel to demonstrate what may well happen when an individual has the opportunity to discover the true word of God, a gift which came to Daniel and which he was able to use to his great benefit and comfort.

Val is a lady with very wide life experiences, now in her later years she has had the energy and inspiration to put her thoughts and dreams to print. It would be her fervent wish that this book and her other works will lead others, similar to Daniel to a much more rewarding and stable life, a life in the knowledge and love of God which brings about true purpose, understanding and peace.

Denis Brown

FETTERS OF A MIND-SET

Whatever we do in a day is worthless- unless it passes the Judgment of God.

'On barren ground we do but spill the Word of God...'

Matthew 19: 26 CEV

Jesus looked straight at them and said, 'There are some things that people can't do, but God can do anything'

This book is dedicated to those like Daniel Steppe, who have recognized the importance of their first glance through the Holy Bible, and know they need this most precious book in their lives?

When following the lead of Jesus Christ, and the Holy Bible there will be many words repeated, by me and thousands of others, those who preach, evangelize, write or just in their daily conversation. I have used words from teachings, words from Bible School lessons, and public meetings, all these were made available to the public for teachers like me, who believe the Word of God is for everyone.

It is for encouragement, and is the same today as it was, the first time it was spoken out.

There are no circumstances or references to anyone else apart from Daniel and his writer.

Please disregard any situations which may be likened to your own.

As you are the reader, you are the interpreter...

A MESSAGE FROM DANIEL

I acknowledge the caring of those who supported me while telling my story, and I ask my God whom I was ignorant of 'in the beginning' to use it as an instrument bringing Glory to Him alone.

For those lost and downtrodden who have found the 'Written Word of God' is a 'Word' to live with not as a book on a shelf, but in your very depths, this is for you.

It is also for souls who have the Spirit of God dwelling within them thus freely sowing the love and peace of God from satisfied hearts.

There is no way my narrative on the Bible would be in print without the encouragement and love from true brothers and sisters who already belong to the family of God.

This book has been written from the 'pen of a ready writer', a writer who was willing to listen to words from someone who was seeking the life shining out there, seemingly out of reach.

It is a journey which took me, an untutored Daniel to experience from opening and reading the Bible for the first time to the revelation, 'the boundary between good and evil' is no more than a tissue thin line'.

And all the margins seem to be bordered with love.

With this so simple revelation I received an emotional tug on my heart which showed me there is more to putting a hand out, and taking a book from a shelf.

Carrying this thought in head and mind, this urging from my heart precipitated taking a step further, a step which enabled me to gather as much inner food as possible all from reading and learning the Bible, I was to come into a life of contentment.

Contentment with what I now have, and with whom I now know.

This contentment and understanding has provided for me a very personal trip through a book which has became my life saver for all my daily living.

I was given the privilege of knowing God through 'The Bible', and the privilege of this writing has been given to the writer of my narrative, this writing does not supersede any biblical knowledge, no one can be greater than the creator of all, we are to be holy but we can never be truly Godly.

This story gives an opportunity to all those who read or hear about it, a chance to know the 'Spoken Word' of the Bible and the 'Original Author' of it.

It is in obedience to the original author, and 'His Written Word' I and my writer as vessels of the Lord, have answered a calling and poured out 'His love' for mankind into this work, and to disobey would be for me the narrator, and the writer to die.

For the wages of disobedience, is death.

There is a love in us, which never faltered or deterred us from believing we can live forever in the beauty of the supernatural realm with the 'Word' on earth, for this is the only way total peace and goodwill is possible in this very impossible, cruel, natural world.

Amen

Isaiah 52: 2 CEV

Zion, rise from the dirt!

Free yourself from the rope around your neck.

'FETTERS OF A MIND-SET'
The journey of Daniel Steppe as he unravels the enigma to the 'Word' on a journey through the Seasons
A story of past, present and the future,

'Well Hello. Where do I start?

I will follow advice which has already been written yes, 'in the beginning'.

I am Daniel; surname Steppe, pronounced 'step'.

I am an honest ordinary guy; just one in the crowd, I have never wanted to stand out.

Before we begin our journey together, I want you to know there is a purpose for it; and this is to have you and me looking upward in the crowd, standing out for we are those who want to change our focus, we are those who want more from our life than just being a mere existence. We are those who want to really live.

Usually when a new person is introduced and we are told something about them a question often asked is 'what do they look like?' so I Daniel Steppe will do my best to describe myself. I am not what one would call handsome, I know when looks were handed out although I didn't receive the tall dark handsome profile like my siblings, I know I wasn't behind the door either.

In height I am just a little short of six foot, an average height you could say, my hair is neither fair nor dark, it could be called reddish, and (unlike a certain King I met in **1 Samuel 16; 12** this is from the book we are going to travel through).

For want of better phraseology I will say my hair is russet.

As for my eyes, when I am shaving I see they are dark blue, it has been said they look through you, seeing all your secrets, but don't you believe it, I just see who or what is in front of me, and not always with recognition, I am sorry to say.

Believe me; I am not interested in your life, well not unless you involve me in it.

Everyone has a distinct identity and I am no different, it isn't our name or looks it is our voice, we can be imitated in what we do, in how we look, and many try to imitate our voices, but nobody can mimic completely all the intonations of it, this is ours alone. It is like a finger print.

Were you ever told 'it is not what you say it is how you say it'?

My family say my voice is 'a butter spread voice, smooth with an indescribable gentleness', which is palaver and certainly overdone, I wouldn't go this far and have often wondered if they are speaking with tongue in cheek, I would never describe anyone this way.

I speak quietly and always have, even when angry although my anger is slow to come it can; I have always managed though to get the message across with a quiet voice.

My brothers were rowdy and there were many times I wished I was; for they seemed to get away with far more than I did, the inch I was given, was a mile for them.

It wasn't until we had grown up I realized the quick giving of a mile to them rather than standing firm, was to stop the shouting voices which could be very distracting, not to leave out irritating when they became louder.

It is obvious there is a relationship between us for we have similar features; and this is where the similarity ends, my brothers were upfront people where I preferred to be in the background.

When I was given the opportunity of sharing my journey to the Bible with you, I was filled with a mixture of apprehension and enthusiasm.

My insides churned with an irrational fear, yes it was of man, and there is no other way to describe it. I carried a fear of being rejected.

Excuses came trotting out of my mouth like verbal diarrhea, if you will excuse my phraseology again.

When these excuses fell on deaf ears I changed my tactics and came out with, why me?

Why not you?

I know irrational can exaggerate beyond the pale, everything can climb out of proportion and become a phobic fear in the mind.

__Romans 13: 3__. Says something about this

What I have kept to myself over the years will be written rationally with new situations added, these give me new ways to view the experiences of my unfettered past.

I was so negative; a positive thought never entered my head.

I would be a new target for many people, those who would rather shun than join in this journey; some of these people also are consumed with irrational fear.

I learnt on this journey my not knowing how to deal with fear, showed me I was inclining toward it, rather than attacking it.

Defending oneself is a problem and very negative, for attacking has to be learnt to really sink into the depths of our soul.

Self destruction begins at birth; for we were born into a fallen world. Adams and Eve have a lot to answer for (and thinking on that we would not be here maybe…)

Irrational fear can be overcome with rational thinking.'

__Romans 8: 5, and 2 Timothy 1:7__

The emotions I didn't want to lay claim to have been written down, we all experience them; they are the experiences we may wish had never happened. It isn't the reader's reaction to this journey I feared the most; it was my own emotions for letting someone else read what I considered to be private, very private. This really bound me up; there was no freedom in me.

Psalm 118: 6

I looked at the happenings in my life impartially putting then put them aside, they were someone else's, and by doing this I could turn a blind eye to them, up until now.

I know the truth has to prevail, and I am thankful to say this writing of the past is with the sight of a Believing Believer in Christ our Saviour, these happenings belonged entirely to me they were my own mishaps, and I have taken total accountability for them, strangely at this very moment of revelation I realized a truth, I hadn't want to own them, I wished they had never been, but for the first time I wanted fulfillment in my life, I wanted to fulfill a desire and a purpose, and have someone say in friendliness to me 'I have been there I know where you are coming from'.

I was silently pleading for someone to tell me I was normal!

I don't want to give the impression only good, pure people write their testimonies.

If they were so good and pure there wouldn't be much to write down would there? For we need comparisons, and certainly with the learning of the good and pure. Confessing the past is what testimonies are all about, and with confession a healing balm can spread over us.

Testimonies are life's experiences.

Believing believer or not, what we utter is still telling someone, something.

I know readers will react to this writing, I have already found that out, the writer and proof readers working with it have shown me the letter 'O' with their mouths many times.

Another thing I know for sure, it is on my head if I lead you astray, *Revelations 22; 18-19* I am accountable for what gets written here, and it isn't my intention for prevarication.

As I have said I believe I am an honest person in both word and deed, and I am not saying this to be boastful,

1Corinthians 1: 26-29

We all see ourselves as something or someone and until the lies in our thoughts and deeds are stripped from us we will never be a true self for others to see.

The truth now is I want to provoke you to jealousy. ***Acts 17: 5,*** I want you to rush off and buy a Bible before you finish reading this story or take the dusty one off your shelf.

This is what my story is about; it is a journey of discovery it is a journey of purpose.

I admit my intentions have changed, for at the beginning of this writing I was unable to say the word Bible' without feeling embarrassed. Probably the other way of looking at that remark is I felt guilty.

I called it 'the book', and many other names like 'red book', 'his book', and I would silently point at it. I thought I would be able to skip through it; if I had there would have been no comprehension of the truth and facts between the covers. Yes I found the word Bible hard to say comfortably.

I would get choked up have a lump in my throat stopping the word 'Bible' coming out.

I kept well away from the subject, and talked about everything else; for frankly I didn't understand what was really going on, I didn't understand I was being drawn by a magnet to something I didn't know what, I was being called just like Samuel, I was being guided by a hand that was unseen.

I believe now the Bible came into my life for a purpose, to take me on a journey, into a promised land.

A journey I see now would have had no purpose; it would be just words without any real meaning, a journey not even worth the paper it was written on.

I am not ashamed of this fact and can see a funny side to it; it is like the rubber tyre one takes swimming, it could be used to save a life, something to hold on to, some could dive neatly through it and some would miss it completely, and I was missing the whole meaning completely.

If it had been said I was deliberately running with attitude using attitude for the purpose of provocation to draw curiosity, I would have run a mile. I would have removed myself very smartly from the scene being created if I thought I was being devious.

Thinking on that, why not use your attitude if it works for good?

I had mind sets!

Don't we all?

Some have taken longer than others to get out of my head; for they seemed set in solid concrete.

One such mind set, the Bible was only for those who preached, and as this let me off the hook, I didn't have to think about it.

This book was not for a man like me, it was for the man who stood up in front of a church congregation and let forth a blast of words not always understood by the many people in front of him.

I had experienced this, I knew some would go home looking and feeling mystified as I had, the one thing they all knew though their good deed for the week had been done, and they also knew they had been seen doing it. *Matthew 6:1*

Sadly, I have found while working with others there isn't any real understanding of what is between the covers of the Bible, and the stories we repeat are just stories, and like me at the beginning they are considered 'an enigma', a total mystery. The mind has been fettered. The chains fettered around your ankles are around your thoughts, and yes your deeds.

There has to be more there just has to be.

My heart was moved into solving the mystery, and to seek understanding of what is needed in this life; I had to seek so this mystery could be unfolded within me for others.

Seek and you shall find

'You have met me now; have you felt a fisherman's hook?

Are we going to continue on together?

My description of myself, it was boring huh?

I said I was ordinary and as I read back yes truth has prevailed. The portrayal written is how I perceived myself 'in the beginning'.

I was just an everyday kind of person, nothing other than one of the crowd.

Do we really notice evening when it comes, or have we been so busy getting things done in a rush through the day, it is upon us before we realize?

I suppose we have become so familiar to this happening it is habitual.

Day following night.

I do not want to talk a walk letting it be a habit; I want to walk a book, it is the Bible's magnetism we are going to unravel, a walk to a book.

We are going to travel through this walk together, not page by page of the book, for everyone will learn it with their own understanding, we are going to travel to a book, and so we can hold this book in our hands, and then let it become the habit, a habit with a purpose in our lives.

This story of mine has a purpose of giving you some understanding to a fact there is a definite need for total understanding of The Bible', and the why?

'For to know the 'Bible', there has to be understanding of whom, 'The Word' is.'

Daniel takes a breather here!

We can now ponder on our first footsteps into the unknown world of Daniel Steppe!

Dear reader, what are your thoughts?

And may I ask?

Is Daniel doing himself an injustice?

He said there hasn't been anything startling so far.

We cannot deny the fact he certainly has a purpose;

It is difficult at this time to find the correct words to give explicit clarity of his description, but there certainly is something about Daniel which cannot be overlooked.

Daniel is very real, and although unseen his presence immediately lets you know he is different somehow.

It doesn't come from his looks; it comes through his personality which can be felt.

His moral fiber is predominantly obvious for one can feel the within.

Many carry an invisible aura, a light shining from within, and those who do so are more oft than not totally oblivious to this fact they do not see the Spiritual realm within themselves. They are unaware of it in their life; for it is part of them.

Being unaware of this aura within they are usually unaware of it as anything other than being right, how one should be, and yes, it does make a difference to someone's appearance.

Daniel and those who carry an aura are like this. It is a natural phenomenon to them.

They do notice those who do not shine though.

The 'aura carriers' do so without a boastful pride. As written it is part of their make up they have no need to be anything other than themselves.

I found out very early in my work with Daniel, that he was unable to enter the room without me knowing.

Even when he stood in the shadows, I would know he was somewhere near.

Good for me, a bit tough on him though!

'Birds of a feather will flock together'.

Daniel loves reading he likes to hide himself in the pages of a book whether it is interesting or not, for he once confessed he didn't have to socialize when reading!

What a cop out, who would have thought this?

He did!

Have you?

I Have?

Daniel being an avid reader becomes invisible sometimes as once I was to experience the visible man becoming invisible, and his disappearance almost caused me an upheaval, it was in an airport mall while, filling in time waiting to board a plane.

I pulled myself out of screaming negativity, changing my focus and became positive, all was solved; he was at the book stall totally oblivious to everyone so engrossed in a book I had to shake him to get his attention.

Initially when he told me about his love for books I felt a stirring within myself, you may feel this same affinity, it is the meeting of kindred spirits, and over a period of time we found we were in tune in more ways than one.

With me if I am not reading for pleasure or searching for knowledge for this is what my reading is often about; I will be writing pouring out, doing gardening, or cooking, the latter two I find somehow therapeutic.

Daniel admits to picking up books wherever he goes, he browses through old book shops, buying left right and centre, some books he will read straight away, many he will leave for the rainy day syndrome.

Who doesn't put books aside for later on, never ever getting around to actually reading them, and as Daniel explained, 'it is a possessive thing for I like owning them' this explanation was for me as well.

There are so many books put on shelves never to be taken out, that is until someone else does the big spring clean after the owners demise into bigger and better, or they have moved on to live in a new lifestyle, with the decision it would be beneficial not to clutter up, and in doing this many pleasures like books are left behind.

It is so easy to take something for granted when it is part of life's automation, and most of us who can read do take this fact for granted.

Daniel, and I am sure you do as well even in this modern age know many who are unable to read, we know it hinders them from doing normal chores if instructions, are to be read first. Daniel wants to find some way to help these people.

When he said this there was shocked surprise, this unsociable man who had to be coaxed into introducing himself in the beginning, actually had social thoughts!

When did this happen?

There are many who take reading for granted, and if you are a reader with no purpose you will know it makes no difference what you read, the newspaper will be sufficient, and this will no doubt be just scanning over the births, deaths and marriages.

The old excuse, I haven't the time I am too busy to read is the most used.

Nowadays even the deaf can hear and the blind can read.

We can learn Sign Language and Braille in a natural world and neither is considered to be unnatural.

We see what is in front by using our fingertips and a hand, letting them take the messages to our mind, having the scales removed from ones eyes which is from the Bible and explains the spiritual realm has a different meaning.

We learn to hear and see from our hearts to get understanding of the spiritual realm.

2 Corinthians 4:1-6

As you read Daniel's introduction you may be able to see him, is it the same way he sees himself?

We glean from his description a wanting to be seen as an ordinary person, whatever an ordinary person is?

Ordinary does not mean we can overlook him!

As we read on we will see he is a natural with a genius mind, this has been gifted to him, a gifting which becomes an inheritance for his future, he is going to use his gift and we are going to reap from what he sows, and then we ourselves can go out sowing a crop for a new harvest.

As the journey continues we will see this ordinary man change and become humble.

Maybe we will change as well!

Daniel becomes not just Daniel, he becomes an imitator, he emulates the God of the Bible, *Ephesians 5:1*, and he expects this from us.

From his understanding he will eventually see where his gifting comes from, and then he will be able to give out to others in full.

Praise God all comes from our Creator.

Daniel, is doing just fine he is starting to allow us to love him, and hang in here we have only just begun.

He has shared what he looks like, which is as he sees himself on the outside, and as we continue learning his likes and dislikes we will see what he looks like on the inside. Huh?

As Daniel and I continue writing this journey together, it becomes very evident everything is for a reason.

The journey we are writing is definitely for you.

THE FIRST SEASON
"Autumn"

Daniel wanted to start his journey in autumn; the season when leaves wither and fall, allowing all the trees to take rest.

This rest is for both deciduous as well as evergreen trees; the temporary and the permanent.

Daniel wants this journey to be remembered and after the necessary surgery we will need, he wants it and us to be an evergreen.

He wants everyone who travels with him to become a spiritual evergreen.

Every tree takes sap back in autumn to the main source of feed, their deep roots.

Autumn is the season for giving back to the roots, the cherished love and peace they have faithfully been feeding on through their display of beauty.

The beauty we have enjoyed through the past spring and summer.

From the trees beauty we have pleasure, and from their branches we see there is a balance, there is shade from the sun's heat, supplying protection to the earth.

And this shade which covers the ground above the precious roots, giving protection to the little creatures to survive, and we mustn't forget also the little creatures living just below the earth.

Daniel says 'the way the seasons change can be seen to happen with a natural ease, and I find I am changing as well and never more so than this particular autumn'.

We all need rest and this season gives rest to the weary. This is the season for shedding and storing up for the long cold season ahead.

It is not just 'a once in a lifetime' season, the 'now' autumn where we have started our journey. There will always be leaves falling as autumn comes round again. And as the leaves fall whether a slow flutter one by one or in fast moving crowds there is a story.

When the wind blows strongly the leaves are shredded off the trees in big clouds, acting as signs for us, they have caught our attention, and we become aware there could be a storm brewing, and we have rain.

If the leaves just fall gently we are see something different, it is our response to these awesome sights where we see a message. For every action there is a reaction, profound but true.

The word autumn is somehow beautiful, and to Daniel it means so many things, the days become shorter and there is a longer reading time in the evening, and yes it is 'harvest time' a time for gathering up stores.

The animals start collecting food ready for their hibernation, the men reap their crops, and the women are making jam and preserving fruit, storing up for the coming winter as well as the following seasons, this is until once again, we are back to a new year, and a new autumn.

What goes round comes around again.
'There is a season for everything'.
The calling has begun

With it being harvest time Daniel was to find he was facing a new situation, he thought he was hearing a voice, a persistent voice.

And he asked himself, 'am I really hearing a still small voice, or is it from an inner desire deep within me'?

Then, 'do I heed this voice, or do I ignore it?'

Usually if it is our sub conscious thoughts, we can deal with it.

This wasn't the same, Daniel felt as if he was speaking to a real person one who knew him.

Like personally?

Although he wasn't pressured, he was very definitely being called, called to come out of his cave, and start preparing ground for the following harvest.

There was a new crop to plant.

The following conversation ensued.

Daniel saying, 'why, do I have to come out of here, I am very comfortable?'

The voice, 'it is time to come out of the cave of your self destruction and share your life with others. It is now your time to receive and give out, joy'.

Daniel; 'Why is it me who has to share a life, it only covers thirty years?'

The Voice; 'Why not you, I have chosen you above others?'

Daniel; 'As I see it my life doesn't appear to be exciting, not enough to make a difference to anyone else'.

The Voice; 'And who are you My Arbitrator?

This is for me to decide. It is time for you to be planted in my garden, to bear my fruit and for me to live in your house'.

Psalm 92:13-15.

'You will be planted beside still waters, and have fruit in all seasons.

You will be planted not by man, and by me you will be rewarded as the blessed man I have chosen'.

As Daniel related this to me, he never once questioned whose voice it was.

John 10: 3.

He knew instinctively the voice calling him was the same voice heard by many others from the beginning of creation.

This was the same voice which told Moses to bring the people out of Egypt.

It was the same voice who chose to call people from their comfort zone and go on a journey.

The voice Daniel heard within himself belongs to the giver of 'Eternal Life'.

It is through obedience we receive relief from the boredom of a daily routine, and Daniel was like so many just living because he could, becoming immerse in a dull existence through not knowing any other.

If you don't know any other way to live, it could be likened to hiding in a cave.

You are in the darkness, and the still small voice which spoke the words, 'what doest thou here?' is going to call out at the right time and you will only hear it at the right time. Yes, you will hear His call.

It has already been written of someone who hid in a cave and this person was called out by those very same words. 'What doest thou here?'

1 Kings 19; 9.

Daniel was being called to share with others his experiences so those chosen to read his story, so please take heart, and develop into lovers of the 'Word' from the Bible' and learn who 'The Word' is.

Not was, 'is'.

His sharing did take him and now you, on a journey through a doorway into the 'last days' where you, like Daniel can change your, negative attitudes to positive ones, and in doing so can forever share with all those around, planting of the positive purpose seed, now starting to germinate within your hearts.

Falling Leaves

There were so many things Daniel had to overcome before he picked up the reins and became serious about the sharing of his true story; and these were dealt with at such a speed he felt as if he was on a roller coaster.

He had to find someone who would put all his past, present as well as his future dreams, on to paper.

He would have to remove the mask he wore and talk openly to someone he didn't know, it had to be someone who wouldn't judge him, and ask 'Who are you? What have you done? Are you important?

Is my time worthy of you?'

It is a fact of life everyone has a story, we all have experiences, this is part of growing up, some will be told, and some will be left untold, many of the untold should have been, and in the same vein there are many told that shouldn't have been.

Life again, huh!

If you hear a voice calling you to share your story, there will be without doubt someone out there who needs to read it, and if you are unable to write it yourself, there will be someone who is waiting to hear from you so they can do the writing.

An unseen preparation will be in progress before you received the idea of sharing your testimony.

There is nothing boastful about it; the idea was put in the little book 'in the beginning of time'.

When a blueprint is being laid down a plan is put into action.

In humbleness seek out the person already chosen for the writing of your confession.

When I first met Daniel I was minding my own business at a meeting and our introduction was to say the least very interesting.

A man almost threw himself down beside me, then turned and said 'I have seen you before haven't I?'

He had some papers in his hand 'I know it is you who will write this' he started waving them about, and then he said, 'I can feel you are different some how'.

Well excuse me!

Here are two people sitting beside each other at a meeting when suddenly one starts up with the worn out phrase 'don't I know you'?

This guy was so wound up he couldn't stop talking.

Yes I am a writer and he chose a nosey one, I knew he had a story to tell just by listening to him, no doubt with my mouth wide open!

I had never ever physically seen this man before in my life and here he was saying he knew I was going to write for him.

Did he know I was a writer; was there a sign on my back?

He said to me 'My name is Daniel Steppe; I believe you already know about me'.

Ha, ha, keep reading; I actually did understand what he was telling me.

There is nothing really odd about it; I had many weeks ago at a meeting through a vision seen a man's face, he had papers in his hand and he asked me to write for him.

I forgot about it as I did with visions, letting them come to me in the reality, it wasn't until Daniel introduced himself it all came back, I remembered I had seen his face before fleetingly.

It was now face to face contact, I realized what he was saying, and remembered the vision of a man, yes it was this one beside me waving papers.

I was chosen, not because I am writer of the year material, I do not lay claim to a title.

I know I was called, I have been chosen to do the work on earth many, many times, the work which has already been done in Heaven, and I was chosen by a much higher commander than two mere mortals.

We eventually chose a time to meet, and as the door opened for the journey to begin, there was a build up of excitement within me, and I was the ready listener who was going to use her fingertips for Mr. Daniel Steppe.

Who hasn't had problems, the giving out of them as well as our thoughts takes a lot of courage, telling the secrets of the past was something Daniel had never experienced before; he liked to keep himself to himself. He has already implied this to us.

He started to mutter quietly on the defensive 'What could my life mean to anyone?'

As a mutterer, Daniel was the worlds best, and it didn't take me long to realize he knew his mutterings were heard, he also knew full well, they were distracting.

It was a defense mechanism; one we all use at sometime or other.

Obviously he needed reassurance and this was to become one of my constant chores.

Many times it was who needs who?

I was to stop him taking the path toward a membership in the S. Double P. club [self pity party]; he finished with 'who would be interested in anything I have to say'?

Plenty are waiting, so let's get on with it!

This was the only time Daniel blatantly behaved in the 'S Double P' manner, and although he continued with his muttering it was with a different tone, usually to finish a sentence for me which could be equally distracting.

Needless to say his story was put onto a screen, and doing so was to become a barrel of laughs! Definitely not all the time we must say.

Each day while writing and getting to know Daniel I was to become aware he had many very strong idiosyncrasies, did he ever?

He pointed out to me once, I had them also. Huh!

This could have been an obstacle, growing out of all proportion as we continued; fortunately neither of us allowed this to happen and we overcame each one with laughter.

He did go off on sidetracks a few times there was a pattern here as well, when ever we were talking about a personal issue he would start muttering something completely different. Don't you love him for being Daniel?

I realized he was trying to control me, to lead me astray; the reason of course was a touchy one and in this particular area Daniel needed be cleansed and tidied up. He had to give it away.

Emotions

His speaking out was the confession needed, although Daniel was to learn the full extent of confession from our past, it does need repentance, to be successful.

Confessions are not a temporary sticky tape; confessions need healing from the divine medicine chest to be completed.

One day he said, 'I feel as if I am on the edge of a cliff. Do you know the feeling?'

<u>Daniel wanted</u> his day, to be exactly as <u>he wanted it</u>, it had to be the way <u>he planned</u>, and he meant everyday, he was starting to realized although still having a choice there was another hand on the gear control lever; this became a real issue to him building up over the weeks, and he became contradictory with himself and me, he became awkward to say the least.

He was two people, one in the open, and one hidden; it was a game of hide and seek, with Daniel the only player.

One Daniel wore a mantle of the positive; the other Daniel wore a mask of negativity, unfortunately through his untutored thinking both of these clothed him in self righteousness. For our journey to progress Daniel's attitude to life had to change from thinking only about him, as yet he never thought about anyone else, you may think otherwise, but remember he is telling us his past.

Daniel had so much to learn, and by walking in someone else's shoes, one can do so.

The shoes Daniel had to put his feet into were his future ones; in this way he would be able to see clearly into his past.

He could look back without reliving it.

He could look back and remember it as experience.

The best way to start seeing oneself is to put on new **forward** shoes and then look back at the experiences of the past.

There is a saying to know where someone is coming from we are to walk in their shoes, this may be a fact, in truth though if there is no judgment in us why do we need to put on someone else's shoes?

There is only one pair of sandals we are to put on our feet, and they are the sandals of peace spoken of 'as the shoes of the gospel'.

Sandals worn by Jesus, from the Bible

As yet Daniel hadn't taken his past shoes off, it did happened and until then there was no depth to his thinking, he still wanted to benefit personally from what he was doing, and there was certainly no permanent evidence of him having softened although there were glimpses. It is all about choice.

He felt the writing of this book was an order, yes he knew it was a divine calling, but he hadn't come to terms with it being **'the blueprint is mine; the choice whether you go along with it is yours My child…'**

Daniel had yet to learn and believe on 'choice' what we do is always from our own choice, and we all have to learn our reason for wanting freedom.

We do have freedom of choice. Good or evil, right or wrong, white or black.

Maybe we have to learn how to spell.

Choice is spelt, C H O I CE, not, S E L F.

Our actions are from our decisions and they stem from our personal choice.

Telling any part of our life is for many a new experience, Daniel had agreed to share all of his, and he was confessing his emotional upheavals twice, yes twice, first to me then to you, and he had no idea where to start.

There is irony in our lives for as each day ends; we notice what we should have done and where we should have been.

We also see what shouldn't have been done.

Every day can end in peace with our acceptance of knowing we did make mistakes, and from these we have learnt; we can carry on into a new day making the same mistakes never learning the key to freedom is never repeating them.

As soon as something is pointed out to us, we are no longer ignorant of it, so making the same mistake in the knowledge it is wrong, has us being nothing other than sinful.

If we are walking with God we will know it is a sin, and if we do not know God there is no knowledge of anything other than sin.

We are not there yet though so this learning is premature.

Daniel started telling me about 'yesterday', which he had not enjoyed, and he saw my look of amazement, the mouthing silently of the letter 'O' I suppose.

There were many times I was glad he couldn't hear my thoughts which were, 'this is going to be a long work for sure'.

He said, 'well where does one start'?

Daniel's sudden look of insecurity; had me wanting to hug him.

He said 'I feel as if my security is being challenged'.

And for a fleeting moment I knew he had seen what was, and what was going to be, he had seen his life as it was and knew without a doubt it was going to change, and like all those who like to categorize and analyze their lives before they move on, Daniel wanted to know why his life was going to change and what for.

There is no mystery here, it is understandable for anyone who walks through the doorway of a changed routine, and anyone who comes out of a comfort zone, there has to be some understanding of the uncertainty which goes with it, for when it does there is an immediate release, removing the advantage the unknown can have.

Where do we start?

Where else?

In the beginning…

This is the start of our autumn change

The dropping of dead leaves, for people it is the shedding of bondages they are our dead leaves; at last there is the understanding we cannot move forward with garbage, we must have a purpose to travel, we must recognize what is stopping us from moving forward, we must learn what it is which keeps us wandering around in a wilderness of no-man's land. Wandering around in the desert of temptation.

It is important to know where we are going, and what we must do to get '**there**'.

We must be aware of everything around us, and most importantly we must be aware of which road we are walking on, for if we don't know this, how will we know where, '**there**' actually is!

Daniel over the past years had learnt to keep his emotions tightly controlled.

His own rules were to keep a blank face have no expression, to never show emotion ever, to never let anyone know his thoughts.

If emotion showed through, his personal secrets were out, he thought!

Live in darkness had been his motto.

This is very unhealthy thinking, for a healthy body.

Daniels' mood swings were well covered up; if it wasn't for the taut lips, nobody would recognize an obvious sign of distress; his lips went into an unnatural tight line; this tight control kept people at a mile long arms length.

I just ignored it and carried on. it was nothing but vapour to me.

Anything to do with 'ups and downs' in our lives can be the reason for mood swings and Daniel felt his reasons were the best of all; these reasons were to be released as we went back to his teen years.

Daniel relates his story to me.

When he was eighteen, he felt as many teenagers do, if they didn't fit into the mold of their siblings, with this it can appear as if their family picks on them. He believed he had a hard time; he believed they were against him. He believed it was the black sheep, in the 'black sheep syndrome'.

There are many young people at the same age who feel this parental rejection usually through misunderstanding.

Daniel's family admitted they had difficulty in understanding his attitude to life, and he definitely had no encouragement from them, when he mentioned what he wanted to venture into.

It wasn't possible a son of theirs would want to do something so unreal and ridiculous, and his father was very strong and extremely verbal in his protests against it.

The cultural way of family tradition is imposed upon us from birth; we have a family's cultural tradition instilled in us and it begins in the family home.

As we grow up the tradition in who we are is continued through to the people who live near us, for they see what and who we are in our neighbourhood.

2 Thessalonians 2:15, 3:6

In conservative areas traditional culture can make us very narrow in our views of life.

There is nothing to give a balance of softness toward it. It can be considered snobbishness, for there is no humility.

Low self esteem is not the same as humility, and is often mistaken for it!

Cultural tradition can be a stumbling block, and it was to be for Daniel, leaving a sour taste in his mouth. *1 Peter 1:18*

A sour taste which showed his pride had been really hurt. I could feel his hurt, but couldn't say anything about it though; he had to speak it out, to start the seeking of his own release from it.

He continued 'I had no interest in the family business of furniture making and restoration'. 'My great, great grandfather had started this business from making a chair in a small shed at the end of the garden; this venture developed through the generations, and by the time

I was eighteen a world renowned Furniture Company had been established turning out, I have to admit beautiful furniture, sold through the demand of clientele.

The demand from the public for the quality of furniture manufactured, eventually over the years kept it a sound viable business'.

'Automatically all sons followed in the footsteps of their fathers, from generations before and before. They went into the business with no exceptions, and no argument would be accepted against this family cultured tradition.

When I said emphatically, I wasn't going to follow tradition; all hell broke loose in the Steppe household.

What happened then was almost a feud, with my family nearly coming to blows'.

'Parents against parents, children against parents, brothers against brothers, a silent war, a silent fight, for only one parent spoke his mind'. My father as head of the family was the voice, and the rest of us stayed silent. Each had a grievance held within though'.

Daniel's father made up his mind he was right this was a tradition going on since forever.

There was no leniency for anyone who dared to want a different occupation.

It was to end in a way only my father could have thought out'.

'Through our family connections, let me tell you', Daniel said with tongue in cheek emphasis,

'I was sent to a furniture company overseas to do an apprenticeship in furniture craft, my father would not, and could not believe I wasn't interested in his company, he thought I was going through a phase of knowing better than him, all the family men as they grew up, wanted to be furniture makers, there had never been any question about it.

I didn't want it not one little iota and said so'.

Anyway it was all arranged and as it was easier for me to go than stay to fight, I went.

My brothers never received the privilege of this extensive training; they just meekly entered the business without argument'.

'As I remember back, they meekly accepted with never a word of wanting to do anything else.

They have told me since I was lucky to be given a choice.

It wasn't a choice though!

Ironically, I was sent to another family business, and from the very lowest position of tea maker, my apprenticeship began.

There was no difficulty learning the trade, I suppose it was to be expected I had a natural aptitude for building. Being a carpenter is what we all do when we are building, when writing we are building a story.

And if we lie to another, we are building on the lie.

I must admit I was a little shocked when my chairs looked like chairs. My thinking was all askew I didn't want to build, I thought I would be hopeless at it, not so as it turned out.

I could see the natural skill; I myself was like a rough piece of wood I was to be chiseled and shaped and all the rough edges sanded and polished off.

The rough edges had nothing to do with the trade; they were from my oversize attitude.

Looking back I can see the chip on my shoulder would have made a dining room suite, it is a wonder I ended up as I did, a furniture maker and qualified designer.

Using wonderful raw wood and ending with a bedroom suite, or a wall cabinet.

I know my parents didn't understand what I really craved to do; and it didn't take me long to realize my timing was wrong. I had no insight to life, although the first chair produced I have been told was made by my great, great grandfather in rebellion, and for no other reason he was laughed at when he shared his dreams with his father'.

<u>What goes around comes around</u>.

'It was not acceptable for me to enter into a totally new field of work, one considered to be non profitable, and a whim, although I went on to do other things, this desire never left my heart.

As I worked through my apprenticeship I was to learn my designs were classed as unique and were well sought after, I was encouraged and allowed to put any of my pieces on the market in my name, with one stipulation they had to be a 'one off' not to be repeated for ten years. Being young and taken in by the verbal admiration I had no problem with this, ten years is nothing but a decade.

From a piece of raw wood, to the buffing of the last drop of oil a final work of art went out into the factory show room. There should have been satisfaction, but I never experienced it, not even when my designer furniture was sort after; I had accomplished this craftsmanship with an inherent skill and I just got on and did it.

I made whatever was requested, there was elation from those around me, even the fact my designs had people rushing to buy them had no effect, there was none of the elation I was expected to feel'.

<u>It is better to eat humble pie, rather than let it choke you!</u>

'Looking back now I know this was not humility, but plain arrogance', Daniel laughed as he went on, 'and I can never deny I had a skill for the work I wasn't interested in'.

'In truth as I have said, it is all about timing and what I had set my heart on wasn't for then, it would have fizzled out for I didn't know anything and wasn't ready'.

'My designs were easy for me to make and I was able to produce them quickly and eventually I received an honour for the one off designs, which led me to being offered a permanent position with the company'.

We can get blown up by our own petard, by becoming boastful; this position was not for me personally, the reality is it was the company who would benefit. I was like the entire employees, paid a wage.

Many events come to my mind as I go on the memory trail, peoples materialistic behaviour is one, greed for wanting something not really needed; it all stems from 'someone else has one'. I was being the instrument for people to get what they didn't need.

Who is being judgmental?

I want to be an instrument in giving out to people what they do need; I want to be an instrument showing there is something waiting for them, and for them to realize they want the missing link to a clean living life'.

I, as the listener and writer wanted to say so much here, but this story is Daniel's, so on we go.

As he continued, 'it has never changed; people still want what someone else has. Will this ever change'?

'There is another dimension too, companies lead and follow this demand, and the reality is customers are encouraged to want their wares; it is survival for the company who also wants to survive, and buyers bring in wages.

We eat from the manufactured table, but it is money which puts the food on it'.

Daniel was like an over wound clock ready to snap, and I thought I was going to get a lecture, but didn't, I sat listening taking notes with bated breath, and feeling surprised again at the fire which was exploding in him.

He went on with some old fashion wisdom 'I thought as my talent could only be intrinsic, inherent, I would have to use it within my Father's company. The loyalty thing I suppose?'

There is a silver lining in everything

Daniel while he was overseas and filling in the off duty time, decided to extend his education so he studied two more subjects, public relations and business.

'I wasn't really serious and let these subjects stretch out over the three years, I received an honour and degrees in both, how do these things happen are they natural aptitudes or a gift, and if so of what?

And from whom does it come from?

'Some say when we study we are cramming our head full of things not needed, if we are led to have education in a certain area I believe there is a definite need to study it, we are to step forward into the age of today, each morning, giving us more insight as we walk along the path of righteousness.

Anyone downing education may be in need of it! Everything we are led to study will be used, to be sure.

Daniel had another O.E. 'overseas experience' one he related to me saying, you write about it. Obviously there was a fence to be mended here, a bridge to be built as it is written down and he reads about it the healing will begin.

Things fall into the right order of significance within our thinking.

Daniel had a tender love experience, his first and he said it was going to be his last emotional relationship.

It was all on, and then it was all off.

This was certainly an area which Daniel needed to look at.

Having no sisters he didn't have home knowledge on girls and this girl he had put on a pedestal.

Pedestals can be unstable and not good places to be, even if a relationship has the qualities of a strong structure, it is inevitable there will be a fall, either for the one who you put on it, or the one on it. In this case both.

Either way it can be pride before a fall.

Girls for Daniel now are friends, not girlfriends. There is no 'getting to know you' anymore, and he actually goes jaundice when this episode is mentioned.

The only women in his life has been his mother who was resigned to living with a family of men, an aunty or two who were only seen on the rarest of occasions.

Daniel chipped in 'Although being very feminine my mother was naturally shy and not one to show her sweet femininity off, she was woman all the way through'.

'I do not speak for anyone else, but my mother was very sweet and courageous, she never left anything undone, doing all she said she would do'.

'This was so natural to her; if she said she was going to do it she would do it'.

'Her word was her bond. From her my brothers and I learnt to finish any chore we started'.

He has caught me, I am like Daniel here myself for I do not know what to write about this 'on, off' relationship.

He has not admitted it could have been because he was lonely and searching for company, maybe he really felt deeply for this girl, we are never going to know for sure, what is fact and fiction will have to rest within Daniel himself.

He achieved his status as a qualified furniture maker, he had learnt a lot in his years overseas, more than he would have if he had stayed put at home, and looking back he said, 'the breakup of my girl friendship, which I had blindly thought was going to be permanent seemed to be the final straw'.

It was a relationship of affection based on many aspects of the life he was living at the time, and although he had thought it was to be permanent, it was wrong timing once again for Daniel.

'I was only twenty one', he said, 'so I decided to put the last three years behind me, and all my education all my new knowledge and go back home to change my lifestyle'.

The prodigal son.

What had he become, what was he?

He had become the son going back home.

As I listened to Daniel speaking through this episode in his life, his experiences, I understood the deadpan voice and face, it was absolutely expressionless; there was no trace of emotion visible, and this always happened when he had to delve into anything emotional.

With listening and really hearing one can understand, for there are very few who cannot relate to emotional situations with ease, we have all been there.

He admitted to a feeling of being banished, of feeling rejected by his own family, he felt so alone and knew being sent away to learn the family business was his own irresponsibility he had brought it on himself. He had been stubborn thinking only of himself.

He was sent to another country, he had no friends, and no family, he felt it was **'learn, or else'**.

He had learnt to develop an expertise of a skill only he could have, which were like his voice and fingerprint, his alone.

What had it really achieved?

Instead of going into the family business which he had been sent to learn, he chose the '**else**'? What had he really done?

He had put all his feelings into a jar tightened the lid, and then openly rebelled; not doing what his heart desired which something his family had considered non prosperous, and what his family considered he should do was go into the family business. He was still young enough to have parental control and so was sent away to learn the business. On coming back he went off and did something totally boring with nothing for his brain to be inventive with.

This wasn't rest time it was 'I'll show you!' Huh

Just working to live, not the heartfelt work he had wanted to do in the beginning.

Something totally boring and repetitive, any old work would do!

Painting a fence of the past, he was trying to cover all the scars.

There were no winners, huh!

It was through this pour out from his mouth, the screw top jar was released, and with the telling of his past Daniels' emotions were exposed, and the rawness within which certainly needed to be released, was dissected then at last into its proper place everything not needed was put, yes we are talking Daniel's garbage here, the garbage he had collected over thirty years was now being sifted, with all the past soul destroying garbage and removed.

Daniel said, 'my past does come back and rear its ugly head now and again, and once this would have me almost depressed'.

'Yes dear friend', I said.

At last I was able to say something, 'until it is all uncovered and released, brought out into the light into the open it will continue to do so.'

This was the truth for I myself had experienced it.

Daniel is like anyone who has a calling on their life. For those who want to live in freedom, they must look at their past and sift the garbage for it has to be uncovered, and dealt with in the correct and proper manner, so it can be release to the only one who is waiting to throw it away, we cannot do what is needed and it has to be done for our inner peace. If we throw it away ourselves and think it has gone forever we are only hiding behind a false security.

The green pot on the lawn can get covered with dead leaves or snow, but underneath it is still a green pot.

I was looking at him anxiously wondering how he was going to cope with the journey in front, I knew from my own experience there was an easy road as well as a hard one, and Daniel hadn't discovered this yet.

He had not made a choice of which way he was going to walk.

He was still but a babe in arms.

Daniel gave a sigh of resignation, a sigh which was saying 'let's get on with it'. He had resigned himself to this story. All should be plain sailing from now on!

In the short time of being together Daniel had learnt rejection was not his alone everyone gets a taste of it; nobody misses out, yes, all and sundry get a taste of being rejected; and if not for how does one learn without experience, and with out the experience how can it be recognized?

It is impossible to deal with something if we haven't first hand experience of it?

And repeating here, how can we help someone, if we ourselves have not had first hand experience of it? We are only supposing you know all.

2 Peter 17-18

Experience must come first

There is glory in the knowing you are not going to mouth off you are going to speak from you own experience, you are going to speak with knowledge.

Daniel was at this moment in time only thinking about himself. In a life time there is endless learning and it is fortunate we do not have to learn everything at once, our day to day experiences teach.

How we live affects everyone around us, and any decisions we make certainly affects our living. He had no conception whatsoever of rejection can be over come by acceptance, being positive will over rule negativity in all ways, and always.

What Daniel thought he wanted, and what he needed weren't the same things?

What he wanted wouldn't be of much use to him in the long term, he will come to understand this eventually and as we continue, he was gathering strength for what was ahead.

There were many steps in front of him before this could happened, and until this moment he had lived all his life in the barren land his surname suggests.

'A steppe' is a barren landscape in vast continents, it is possible to stand and look out at the horizon many, many miles away, and see nothing just nothing at all.

It would be like walking through a wilderness.

The landscape is totally barren which ever way one looks, our lives can be like this, and there is no future if we harbour a negative outlook within.

As Daniels story unfolds he goes back to the time 'when he became unsettled', he said 'there had entered a deadly boredom within me one which made it impossible for me to relax in my old habits'. This had happen before in his daily routine, then he had just ignore it, only it wasn't the same now, this unrest came more from within him and it was right in his face. Don't you love it?

This feeling of unrest meant business, big time.

His attitude to life was changing, listen to this, he said 'it wasn't me changing at all, everyone else seemed to look different and they were saying different things to me. Everyone I came in contact with had changed toward me'.

Whoa up here, Daniel. Are you sure this is right?

You have just said it is you who became unsettled, so how come it is those around you who have changed? Huh?

How do you know they are unsettled did they tell you this?

As I brought this to his attention he had to admit he was passing the coin over, 'I had become cozy with my life style and didn't believe it needed to change'.

Where he had once accepted the boredom, it had now intensified making acceptance not an option.

Was it my prodding, or an unknown force urging Daniel to grab hold of a memory and find out what was next?

Do we have to remember our past?

Today is a new day rejoice and be glad

'This new day weather wise was cold and dull, not a sunbeam to be seen' Daniel speaking, 'I went to work; hoping I could immerse myself in it, but was bored, I didn't have any of my usual get up and go, even my acceptance to this work had me agitated and bored.

I did what was expected of me on automatic pilot, but where was I, not at the workplace for sure, in fact I was wondering if I had actually come in?'

'As the afternoon was drawing to a close, I decided on my way home to take a brisk walk to clear away the cobwebs, maybe this would help me to clear my mind before I sat down to eat and have my evening read'.

He had already told me his evening read had become a habit over the years, in fact his whole evening was one he looked forward to and enjoyed, he was determined this would never be changed.

I had my tongue between my teeth, thinking thoughts about change and how I had been through it all, and not a just few of my habits removed, every single one had been.

Habit forming went straight out the window forever. I became as nothing, I live for God, and dress not for people but for me. Style means zilch.

Daniel said 'I was thinking with a determination about change as I walked briskly, 'and yes' he said I was muttering 'habitual living keeps me on track.

'As the cold raw air hit my face there was urgency for me to hurry along and leave thinking alone. Why can't I get pleasure out of my everyday programs?' Daniel asked me.

'My walk on the down lands which is one of my favorites gives one a view a panorama out of this world and I didn't enjoy it; I was totally blind to my surroundings.

'I had a quick snack, usually I liked to eat leisurely as you know for this is my way of winding down, I like a drawn out meal in the evenings after my work, but tonight I wanted to read rather than eat, and this put me at odds with myself, I was wondering what was going to be the next thing on the list of strange happenings to me. There must be a reason for these odd things; one doesn't just change for fun, does one?'

He looked as if he expected the answer to jump up into his face, and I was hoping he didn't expect it to come from me.

Where had all his pleasure gone?

As I transcribed Daniels notes I became use to his standing beside the desk, and each time he did this I knew he wanted to add to a sentence.

He would do this and not always patiently I might add, he remembered things which he would spill rapidly from his mouth in case he forgot. There were so many 'Daniels' at times I wondered which was going to be the winner, which was the real one. I knew it had to be the Daniel which peeped out at me with the mischievous grin fleetingly as it was.

There were times when I thought he should leave well alone and throw some things away, but it was his story I was writing, I had to remember it was his confessions.

Daniel, I am thankful to say was always ready with answers to any questions I asked him, and many times I had to ask for more detail so a reader didn't wonder what planet we were on.

We went on like this covering many pages when out of nowhere he said,

'Have we a third party present'?

'We are on our own what do you mean'?

I knew what he was saying; I wanted to know if he did.

'I feel sometimes we are not alone; in fact I have this very strong perception of someone looking over my shoulder'.

I couldn't resist the next 'like you do with me' and we both laughed easing the situation, although the question he asked didn't get answered, it would be answered soon enough, only not by me.

Daniel had planned in his head a story and how he wanted it written, the problem here for him it wasn't coming out on the screen entirely his way. And they were not coming out my way either; my fingers were at the key board but doing what they were told from my heart not my head.

Yes, there certainly was a third party with us.

At last he was learning, not everything goes according to our own plans. There is a saying 'The plans of mice and men'

Daniel was on the fence ready to fall over into another realm where the timing isn't ours.

This journey has us now within the reach of the oasis where Daniel will be able to drink and know the choice to do so was inspired from within him, he couldn't have ventured on this journey any other way.

We may have answered a calling to choose whom we want to be in union with for the rest of our lives on an individual basis, Daniel's story is the same only is being used as a dragnet to bring you and others closer to the 'The Word' mentioned in a book called The Bible.

We may have only glanced at it over the years; now we are being drawn to complete an unfinished work.

The decision on what we do or don't do is still ours, and if we are heading the wrong way there will be a little voice saying

Isaiah 30:21

'This is the way, walk ye in it'

Do you really want to go the wrong way?

Daniel was about to make the choice between 'good and evil' positive and negative, the choice which changes lives.

It was coming closer for Daniel to choose which camp he wanted to live in.

Yes the presence, the third party he spoke about was drawing Daniel closer and was coming at the right time to save him; this Presence was drawing nearer with a determined force.

I am; I am your inner light

Daniel continues with his testimony in a state of awe.

'After my shorten meal', which he said almost accusingly as if it was my fault, 'I was standing in front of the bookcase thinking with a blank mind, and picked out a book with the title 'The Holy Bible'.

'This was the first time in my life as far as I can remember ever looking at a Bible, I did have a small prayer book given to me at school, but everyone got one of those, and like every school pupil not many really looked at it.

The book in my hand meant nothing to me; and suddenly it had become the only book on a tightly crammed shelf.

This book was the only one with the light shining fully on it, and listen you won't believe it, as I tried to put it back I couldn't, it seemed to be invisibly glued to my hands'.

The plans of mice and men

'I had a new furniture magazine to look through and don't you laugh' he scowled, 'I am not interested in this really, but I like to keep in touch also it was free'.

Yes, right! Who was trying to justify his actions?

Excuses, excuses they would have gone on forever if he hadn't been stopped.

'There was no reason for me to go to the bookcase, only there was a strong force encouraging me to so, I was being compelled to choose a book, as I think back this, the 'book' had already been chosen, anyway I felt compelled by an unseen hand'.

I tried to not grin for I believed him when he said 'I am sure I felt a hand'.

Daniel went on, 'I instantly liked the feel of this maroon leather bound book, I read some of the words they made no sense at all just jumbled words, the sentences were an enigma to me, they were indecipherable, and as I continued to peruse, as one often does before they put a book back on the shelf, it was very plain everything within was a mystery to my understanding'.

This same thing can be experienced by anyone who picks up the Bible for the first time. You rack your brains trying to remember if there was anything you had heard about the written content.

There is a blank; nothing tickles the memory to give you any inkling to familiar territory.

Do you know we usually read books we can relate to in some way or other, there seems to be an instinctive pull within us which recognizes what the content is of a book, many choose by the title, or the picture on the cover, as many do by choosing an author, either way there is an instinctive pull.

Daniel did remember a little of his Sunday schooling, he remembered about Noah, for there had been a flood around this time where he lived and he was a little frightened he would be drowned. He remembered other names, what they had done, there was no definite knowledge and what he did have certainly wasn't enough to attract his attention as a very new reader to this book, there was nothing inspiring Daniel to keep him reading on.

He drew a blank he was totally vacant, 'so what is this book?

'The Bible, what is this all about and where do you go from here?' he asked himself.

He said 'I had so many questions running through my head; strange thing is I wasn't confused everything seemed precise around this jumble of words'?

He was looking through me as if he was in another place, his eyes were glazed with past memories, I waited for him to speak, 'I didn't want to read it, and if I did what then?' And yes another sentence, 'what is the point of reading it anyway?'

Then he said, 'is there a point in reading it?'

Instinctively with any book, there is a natural curiosity, which can have us looking closer.

Basically we are an inquisitive lot.

Who knows what the mind needs to pick up on?

Who knows what food Daniel needs; did he need something which his every day life lacked?

There are some who can blatantly sort out the plot of a book by reading only the first two pages.

The Bible does not allow this, there are so many meanings in the words on one page, and one scripture can mean many different things to us the reason for that is we are individuals.

The stories have hidden life; it is obviously a book that has to be read with purpose.

Philippians 3: 15

Show me a book written without a message, I don't believe there is one, every book has something to grasp, however trivial the story may be.

Remember trivia to you may not be to someone else.

Daniel was asking, 'what message are we to get from the Bible?

Is there a message?'

He wasn't asking me, he was asking himself, and then came 'do I need to know?'

He could still remember the prompting from within to carry on reading; he was nodding, and then he said 'yes I was plagued with curiosity, I had been aroused and I definitely wanted to know the answer'.

The answer to most things when living with negativity will never be the same as the one you get when living with the positive attitude. We must seek out; we must find our own personal path and this will either be a smooth hard rock or cobblestones uneven with us stumbling along the way.

Proverbs 3:23

Daniel who was starting to see these things suddenly found something other than self to think about.

Huh! He got there, how about that?

He was thirty years old; and at the age of twenty-one he had decided he would do things <u>his way</u>, in <u>his time</u> never doing anything unless self benefited. He had selfishly thought about no one other than himself for nine years.

Daniel was for the first time thinking about a book which meant until now nothing to him; he didn't even know how it had a place on his shelf.

It had no signature, no name of ownership; it wasn't a present from anyone, and he certainly hadn't bought it.

Someone must have put it there!

Well how else did it get on the shelf in his house?

Many of us only see what we want to, sometimes missing the obvious even though it has been in front of us all the time.

Daniel was thinking about this book, until now there had been no reason to do so, he said 'I was like a statue frozen in time as I stood thinking about it, and then very clearly I heard a quiet voice saying

2 Corinthians 8: 10-15

'What was it you so desired to do when you were eighteen?'

'My heart gave a jump of apprehension, I felt almost scared. I remembered what I wanted to do instead of going along with the family and with the realization came these thoughts, they had never gone away; they had been buried in a place so deep within me.

I had buried them because I had been too weak to fight for my dream'.

'Can dreams become reality?'

They can and do. If you can dream it, you can become it.

If you can imagine it you can achieve it.

'Do I really want to unfold the jumble of words in this book, or do I want to leave them for another day?'

Which is the easiest?

'There was an inadequacy within me, how would I cope with the challenge I knew 'The Bible' was offering me'.

There was a challenge, and if he argued he would be the looser for there can be only one winner in a war.

'Who am I fighting with and against whom though?'

Did he read it, or put it back on the shelf to gather more dust?

Who was his challenger?

Had he suddenly walked into a time zone, was he going to go backward or forward, science fiction stories they speak about time zones, was he in one?

I don't think so.

Was it now his time for the wake up call from another realm?

Were all his unanswered questions at last going to become answered ones?

'Let's be truthful Daniel' he said to himself, for he knew without doubt the time had come for truth.

'What is truth? Who is truth?'

He was starting to wake up to the reality of the world, he said 'The security I built around myself is making me feel insecure'.

The safe world he had wrapped around himself was just a fake, giving out false security once again.

'Yes, be truthful', he said, 'my eyes have been open, only I didn't see a thing until now. I had scales over my eyes and now I see the world is full of promises'.

The mantle of righteousness and the veil of darkness!

Daniel realized there had to be a change from whom he was, to where he was meant to be.

Would he change without knowing, no he couldn't as yet for he didn't know what this change really was going to do for him?

If he had changed from who he was then without knowing he could be led to being dissatisfied with where he was.

There has to be balance.

This could go on forever and Daniel realized he didn't want to be undecided forever; now was the time for him to make the big decision.

As it turned out, he made a life saving decision.

He was muttering to himself again making sure I heard, 'Come on, time to wake up, and get real'.

He muttered on, 'Am I going to wake up to reality and see clearly all I pushed away when I returned from overseas. Will I see clearly what I had buried within myself?

'I know I was arrogant and rebellious, and I know I deliberately ignored things, and I was aware I stumbled, I just wasn't aware it was my attitude toward my past causing me to trip up so many times?'

'Where will the answers come from, someone out there or from this book called, The Bible?'

Come and rejoice for this is the day!

Waking up what is that all about?

Some wake up in the morning and pray, and the doing of this is a natural event for them! They are coming out of the land of sub-consciousness, where they have been dreaming. With dreaming our minds are aware, and if we are not dreaming we have been in a deep sleep unconscious, where our minds have taken time out; we went off duty to the world?

Daniel knew he was waking up to the issues he had been ignoring; he had put these things off for a long time, hiding the issues which needed attention was his way of getting rid of them, it is a sin to leave issues undone, especially when we know they should really be attended to, and this should be immediately we become aware of them.

As for living he was just plodding along, he went to work everyday and the routine he followed religiously had become a routine of, waking up having breakfast, then going to work, eating, taking a walk, coming home having another meal, reading for a while, then back to bed again, and what for, to wake up and go to work again the next day?

His work had become habitual, it was dull, boring and of no benefit to anyone but himself, and all for the money in his pay packet at the end of the week. Ironic isn't it Daniel who only wanted to do things his way only for his own benefit was bored.

Does this prove we need more in our lives than self?

As he spoke about his work he said for the umpteenth time 'there was only disillusionment for me in it'.

Daniel had at long last admitted and not outright I must say his work wasn't allowing him to use his full potential.

He knew he was really letting the benefits of his mastered craftsmanship and his educated degrees stagnate.

He was only putting enough money in his pocket to pay his bills; an issue in itself, he had all he needed, or did he?

Something of importance, he realized his attitude to everything was not needed. He had ridiculed this very thing at one time in others, and now it had come back to bite him.

He didn't want to go crawling back to his parents, begging their forgiveness for pushing them away as he did, he had struggled rather than show love, and being proud people they stayed away waiting for his hand to welcome them back into his life.

He hadn't until the telling of this realized how big the rift was, it was him who severed the contact, and the results had in reality been detrimental to only him, it was he who made up his mind not to take the hand out he was offered on his return from overseas.

Pride is dreadful if in the wrong place.

He owed for nothing and he didn't want to owe anyone. The strict morals on borrowing which he had grown up with were well imbedded within him.

It certainly showed he had inherited this pride as well.

His pride was an issue, and would have to be dealt with sooner than later. Pride brings shame.

He just had enough money to buy his food, without the luxuries.

Who hasn't been there?

Daniel's education was such he could have been the employer rather than the employee.

Giving out orders rather than taking them.

Who was in a rut of circumstances, caused by self?

We have all been in a rut; it is the getting out that can be difficult; to break free one has to look at personal traditions.

The personal bondage we put upon ourselves does so much damage we become so used to living with it, and gradually it becomes a mask which we wear for all occasions not just to the ball.

One must be strong. One must be positive.

Being bold and decisive is something Daniel had never excelled at, it was easier to stay out of view and not make waves, to be on the defensive all the time, always justifying his actions, never attacking.

When we don't make waves? What are we doing?

Nothing at all!

Silence is not always golden.

This became a habit with Daniel in many situations at his place of work, he could have saved the day many times, and he didn't for it was easier not to. There are times to step back but there are just as many times for us to step forward.

There were many times over the last years, when decisions had to be made and Daniel stayed silent.

He knew each time there was a crisis he should have spoken up for the answer was simple and right in front of him, because of his silence he realizes now he portrayed himself as having no opinions. He was there with them, seen and not heard.

He was as if nothing.

His workmates may not have gone this far with their thoughts although there would be without doubt some derogatory comment made about him in the canteen.

The place where all meet and the grievances about workmates and the bosses are poured out.

They drink tea or coffee as a panacea to put back into their bodies a refreshment to restore them for the next shift.

Daniel stayed well away from this for he had never been able to abide the habit of gossip.

Many of us regrettably stay silent; with the results the task becomes more difficult than it should have been.

Omission is another word which can be added to procrastination. Both are sins.

No one looked to him for the answers, and when you do not offer to help, no one is going to ask you for it. Daniels life was very empty, there was no excitement in it, it had all become habitual he never dared to do anything to stand out, until now; in fact as he stood still and took stock of himself, he saw there was more excitement in discovering 'The Bible' than anything else in his life time.

There had been a book on his shelf, a book he had heard about, a book full of history, a book he had never ventured to read. He knew it contained truth and fact, and yes Daniel wanted now to read it.

History he enjoyed reading about. He said 'although I didn't know about some of these people what they had done or who they were; I knew they had really existed. Jesus existed it is a historical fact.

Then he said. 'When my brothers and I were young we did go to a local Sunday school this never developed into anything, for our father who traveled for the business always expected us as a family to go with him.

Staying over was a common thing which could cover several weeks at a time'.

Had he and his brothers in their youth been so sadly neglected of Sabbath education?

He doesn't believe so, he knows they received biblical teaching; and he could only answer for himself, 'when I actually did have this teaching I obviously didn't want to know about it. I do know as all the children around us went to the church hall we had to go as well'.

He really couldn't remember.

Families sent their children for Christian tuition because it was the thing to do.

It was traditional, what they learnt would be a foot step in Christian morality.

It is no different to nowadays, this is a pattern of negative life we only take in what we ourselves will benefit from. Self again!

The book, the Bible suddenly started to draw him to investigate; Daniel seemed to have a magnet pulling him towards it, and having this natural aptitude for learning which he had tried to keep suppressed over the latter years he wanted to know more, and from within there was a slow release of emotional curiosity.

Daniel was experiencing something which could have been aroused earlier, although he admits he was not ready for any of the silent prompting he was now experiencing, and it was this prompting which was making him look for answers to why his life was so very dull.

There were questions building up within him, 'what is the reason and what are the things I should know about, how does the knowing fit into my lifestyle the comfortable one I live in and thought I enjoyed over the last few years?

Did I really enjoy them though'?

Daniel's mind triggered off many thoughts, and he knew as many people do who ask questions he would either get answers from the written words in the Bible, or he wouldn't. Then the revelation; and he knew with certainty all the answers would come from, 'The Bible'.

He told me 'What I did next was a bit odd, for I put the book which was the cause of all my questions and soul searching back on the shelf, with its cover dusted, and in a place where I would be able to see it quickly, for I knew I was going to take it out again.

Oh yes, I knew I would and I did quicker than a flash of lightening.

'The next evening when I sat down for my habitual reading I had in my hand, yes you guessed it, The Bible, and this time I had made a beeline for it, I had deliberately picked it out'.

He was laughing, 'Don't you love me'?

'I picked it out with total awareness I knew which book I had in my hands, I felt the same awareness when I put it back on the shelf.

As I looked at it, I was thinking about my day at work, and the feeling of urgency to get home, I liken it to unwrapping a surprise parcel on my birthday, and by the time I did arrive home I was in a state of trembling anticipation.

I tried to douse the curiosity which was simmering within my body by slowly eating my meal, it didn't work. It seemed as if a fire had been lit, spreading a heat through me'.

What is the importance of, 'The Bible?'
What is with this book?

'This book had never been of significance in my life, it was just a book taken from the shelf initially and somehow it was making its presence known, Daniel said 'I knew it was going to always be with me getting me to incline towards it, there was a gentle pressure which I knew was going to continue unless I read it'.

He didn't know 'The Word' would continue as a presence for the rest of his life a presence along with another stronger more powerful force in a spiritual realm.

Daniel had just come through the first season, the start of transition from his usual reading, to reading the book called,

'The Holy Bible'.

WINTER
Where All the Branches are Bare
Daniel Enters his Second Season.

The Bible opened at *'Isaiah'*.

And in front of Daniel he read from chapters *63, 64, and 65*.

63:13, *'who led them thro the depths? Like a horse in open country, they did not stumble; like cattle that go down to the plain, they were given rest by the Spirit of the Lord'*.

He continued reading

64:6 *'all of us have become like one who is unclean, and all our righteous acts are like filthy rags, we all shrivel up like a leaf, and like the wind our sins sweep us away'*.

Then he read **64:8**

'We are the clay, you are the potter; we are all the work of your hand'.

65:2 *'all day long I have held out my hands to an obstinate people who walk in ways not good, pursuing their own imaginations- a people who continually provoke me to my very face, offering sacrifices in gardens and burning incense on altars of brick;'*

'see, it stands written before me; I will not keep silent but will pay back in full; I will pay it back into their laps- both your sins and the sins of your fathers', says the Lord.
I will measure into their laps the full payment for their former deeds.'

At the bottom of the page,

65:12, *'you did evil in my sight and chose what displeases me.'*

Daniel had known from the moment he found The Bible something or someone was going to shake him, and now he knew there was someone who wanted him to look closely at himself.

He read again, 'you did evil in my sight, and chose what displeases me'.

'How does the author know all about me?'

'If he does how come he has missed the fact, what I chose to do was thrust upon me?'

'What I chose to do was not my own choice. I am talking about my trip overseas and the education I had at the time'.

Well now is the time.

Daniel was at last now sharing in detail his deeper thoughts with me, and once he started he was on a roll.

'There are so many things to put down on paper, and some of them are repetitive, have you found I repeat myself often?'

Have I ever!

It is Daniel who is leading us on this journey, and there is a time and a place for both emphasis and repetition.

I will never forget what it was like when Daniel and I first met when he told me I was going to write his narrative, he was as downtrodden as anyone who lives a selfish life.

It was as if he was sliced in half, one half was downtrodden and wearing dirty rags, and the other half was clean and expectant.

Daniel had the belief from the very beginning his life would change with a book, he thought wrongly though for is not the one being written, it is the one he picked at random from a bookshelf. Meditate for a moment we may have been in this same situation ourselves, and if not we are able to share with Daniel.

Daniel was compelled to pick this book off the shelf.

'But whom was I being compelled by?'

The unbelievable believing thing is Daniel never once in all the time of our writing his journey had any doubt to the authenticity of, 'The Bible'. He never doubted the author was of another realm to the one he lived in.

He knew it was written hundreds of years ago, he knew it had to be written long ago he said 'isn't it strange that a book written so long ago, as it was then, is for now.'

Daniel believed it was for those generations, as it is for his generation, and will be for the next. He believed this as a fact and truth.

The words and their meaning will never change we just have to learn to understand the reality of what is truthfully being said to us.

The 'Word' from The Bible will never change, this 'Word' is like the ever-green tree which never looses its leaves, the words are the sap which feed the root, and for people these roots are the only foundation for a life of quiet peace, they are the foundation we are to stand on. This foundation starts with our moral Christian upbringing.

Another thing which is a certainty, from the moment Daniel picked up this book he knew it was 'The Word' who intended to be fully introduced to him, and also 'The Word' needed and wanted to be the only influence in his lifestyle forever more.

The sentence Daniel re-read made it very clear, and we repeat, although The Bible was written many years ago, the very words enclosed between the covers certainly pertain to nowadays.

Somehow and there was no reasoning for this Daniel knew he had to maintain order from what he was reading, and so he started on a journey within a journey to find understanding and peace? Knowing these two couldn't come from the people around him.

Oh no, they would come from a book called The Bible. The real tutor once the words were installed within his empty cold heart would bring to life a heart filled with the fire of understanding.

Daniel knew all the answers he ever needed for his future were in this book, the book forever near his hand, the book called, yes 'The Holy Bible'.

He suddenly felt exhausted, ***Jeremiah 12:5,*** it was as if he had been fighting a battle with the life which was, as he sat quietly with the book on his knee it was this very moment he was to see how his life should be, his past was being dragged nearer for its clean-up. The leaves of bondage were to be buried forever, and would stay buried unless Daniel focused on them again.

His choice he made silently just like the wind sweeps over us.

Our past must be put in its place, darkness is death, there had to be light in all the traumatic burdens Daniel was carrying.

Darkness of the past must be buried, and the light which gives so much will be the over comer, putting to rest all his fears. 'False Evidence Appearing Real'! F.E.A.R!

The experiences from the traumatic issues he had lived were there to learn from, and through this learning he now had wisdom bringing positive results enabling him to encourage and help others in the same situation.

He can walk forward with no looking back, there is no longer a fear of becoming a hardened pillar of the past, it is easy he found to let go the trauma, and once he had dealt with it in the light from within himself, he found on the outside, the truth exposed the fear it had disappeared.

Daniel will never forget the lessons he learnt, it had been ordained he is going to use each lesson. What reason would there have been for a lesson in the first place if it were otherwise? Everything is for a reason, and relating our experiences will be in the right season.

There is a change upon us.

The thoughts which were now entering Daniel's head were centered in a different area, and it was easy to see he wasn't happy about it.

We were quietly plodding along writing on a smooth roll; and suddenly we had the hic-ups. Daniel was speaking in fits and starts, and his uttermost thoughts were centered on hatred, ouch!

If you want it milder dislike, he said, 'I have never hated anyone'. Did I believe him?

What he said rolled off his tongue so easily; he had never hated any other person in his life, those he didn't get along with he walked away from, but Daniel knew he was lying, for there was hatred in his heart.

For whom though?

'Hate is an emotion, is it not?' he asked.

Well, well, many times I thought Daniel was emotionless, his voice would be totally devoid of natural expression, and one would expect those sharing their experiences to sound tearful or choked up with some emotion.

With Daniel whenever feelings were mentioned or anything to do with feelings, with his own emotions, he would become overtly bland. Utterly tasteless.

Too bland!

Cover up.

Daniel couldn't or wouldn't remember hating himself over the years, or hating anyone else. Huh!

He knew likes and dislikes ruled people, not liking this one, or that one, he heard his work mates talking about their spouses and family in derogatory terms often enough.

Hating anyone would mean emotions and have you realized this would mean Daniel wasn't stagnating as he wanted us to believe.

The heart certainly can deceive, *Jeremiah 17: 9, Amplified*.

Daniel, if we feel any emotion we are alive to something.

Our feelings are our emotions.

It was an emotion which Daniel felt when he opened this new book.

His work mates seemed to dwell on their feelings towards others it was their daily fix, their dislike kept them going.

Daniel asked, 'why don't they stay silent, why do they criticize people all the time?'

I could answer this for only myself; I was once like Daniel, and like him I had to travel a journey to find complete understanding for the same question.

Where Daniel said he didn't hate himself, and I do not believe it, certainly at one time I saw me as nothing other than the lowest form of being. I felt as if the world owed me when I went through my wilderness years.

It is easier to have negative thoughts, rather than face the fact we have fear within us, thus having us in reality blind.

What this does is insult our creator as well as ourselves.

There is a time to become real and know and believe the fear of man is a stumbling block.

Daniel knew he hadn't been a likeable young man before going overseas and it was the same when he came back, he didn't say 'I don't like myself', what he said was 'others don't like me.' Self was blind, huh?

To be liked we must let others see we like who we are.

'Something really unexplainable, as in unbelievable happened at the airport on my return', Daniel went on 'as soon as I saw my parents and my brothers, the ill grace went out of me and the bond of family love took over, it seemed as if I had never left home'. ***Psalm 25:15*** 'I walked back into the chain of love which I had missed while away'.

Daniel was looking at me waiting for a comment.

So many times through this narrative I had to break eye contact with him, you and me are learning about him, and right now he was expecting me to disagree with what he had said.

He actually wanted me to justify his behaviour and his attitudes.

I really understood through the love of my creator, also the love of a husband and family, I have learnt sticking plaster doesn't necessarily allow wounds to heal.

Everything has to be cleansed.

His family had forgiven him for what was considered his rude behaviour and the lack of correspondence over the three years he was away.

This forgiveness from them was immediate; it happened the moment they saw each other.

The lack of correspondence still irks him; he regrets it and knows now it was really rebellion.

His mother would dearly have loved receiving something more than a meagre card at Christmas. 'The ones we love can be the ones we hurt the most'. That popped out of the mouth of Daniel, not me.

He said 'never once did my mother mention the lack of news, she just showed her love, and welcomed me back as the long lost son'.

'My father was the same. Never a cross word came from his mouth once I was back home'.

Daniel admits his brothers, who are now married with children and seemly mellowed, were not as kind initially.

Daniel had never given a thought to what his actions had done to them, he can now see the reality of it, and he said 'probably because I was still being arrogant, I never looked for the truth of what it had been like for them. And from what they have said, they were the ones to bear the brunt of my attitude, and my going away was a release for them.

They were relieved to see me go; it took the pressure off the family situation'.

What it is with attitudes? Huh.

Although timing is the essence, Daniel could have had more sensitivity to his brothers' feelings, and realized just because he was no longer in sight, nothing had changed it was still he, who had argued, and the argument was still there, and stayed there until he returned. 'Yes, it was me who caused the disharmony within my family; and in all honesty I know now it was with selfishness'.

What insight!

He was a little down mouthed here and I could see he had a 'get this bit over quickly' look on his face; because low self esteem had crept in, it was pointed out 'quickly' often important things are left unsaid. His sigh almost moved the papers on the desk.

Confessing is two thirds healing although he didn't see the telling of his soul was doing this. He believed, even though it was his journey the telling of it was for everyone else, not himself.

We must confess if we want to receive the healing.

At this time he did not see it as a healing in progress. This is something he will see as the journey reaches its conclusion after going through all the seasons.

His whole demeanor was changing right in front of me, and as he continued talking about his first time sitting quietly with the Bible he said, 'Darkness is the absence of light.'

I now understand the saying 'out of the mouths of babes', you would never believe it!

Daniel was waking up.

How many times do we think about, 'darkness being the absence of light' has anyone ever given thought to this before turning on a light switch?

Do we automatically just push the button expecting the power to come on?

What do we expect when it doesn't?

What are our thoughts then?

When I asked Daniel about his last comment and why he said it, he just stared at me, and then replied.

'In truth, I do not know why I said it, I just did'.

'There was a picture in front of me', he continued 'a vision, a long narrow track barely visible, it wasn't too dark for I could see tall trees on either side, there was litter under them and this was highlighted, I had a feeling of repulsion, I was appalled at the litter, there was so much and piled so high. I could see this clearly and I could see the shape and size of the trees, they were shadowed, there was dimness'.

Daniel continued, 'on the horizon, I saw a big bright light coming from above it was a ray beaming down on to the narrow track, and you are not going to believe this, it was like it was beckoning me, showing me where to start walking, I knew I was to walk forward, and the words 'darkness is the absence of the light' just came into my head'. ***Isaiah 30: 21***

Well, well who has had a vision?

Already the Bible was sending out messages to Daniel, bringing conviction to him, this book is a must to be read, a confirmation from someone. It is to be read somewhere at sometime, for what follows the reading is our being placed on the correct path, a path of righteousness, and with this comes understanding.

Daniel wasn't bothered too much about the past anymore, he wanted to leave it and go on with something else, he wanted to step into the Bible.

It was me who had the vision then.

If anyone says to you excitement is contagious believe them, Daniels' exhilaration was something to be seen, it hit me and the proof readers with full force.

To ignore the fact we have a past is not right or proper, to remove the tarnish it must be sifted through, as already written the past must be put in its proper place.

Daniel opened, The Bible and read the very first words, 'In the beginning', the reading of those words was all it took to have him throwing away the dead leaves he was aware of carrying, he was exposed he said he 'felt naked with his clothes on I was stripped of everything I didn't need'.

All the loose bark on his trunk which had scores of hiding places for little parasites to eat away at him, never ever allowing him to be anything other than dirty.

They were all crushed put to death by being exposed to the light.

Reading 'in the beginning' was all it needed.

Every single thing not wanted, the rubbish cluttering up his mind, the destroying rubbish, stopping the sap from going back to the roots of foundation, this same rubbish was stopping the sap from renewing his body and mind, and this was being removed through his belief in 'The Word', all was being removed through belief.

The Bible is full of positive words and these words were bringing him to a place of total cleansing. The green pot is going to stay green forever the difference now there is no longer need for it to be covered up with earthly snow to make it look pure.

Daniel no longer needed to wear a mask.

The renewing of the mind, and blessed are we who can have such a journey. Daniel had belief in his Bible, through 'The Word', whom he could not wait to meet face to face.

O that such a journey can but begin;

Daniel starts his biblical journey off in Genesis, the first book of the Bible, and He says, 'I notice the Bible is in two parts the Old Testament and the New Testament, why is this?' then he answered himself, 'it doesn't matter I know I will learn why somewhere on my trip?'

He was grinning at me as if he had a large piece of cream cake in his mouth and extra slice in his hand. His grin revealed a real joy. Daniel was on a trip walking into the Shekinah Glory of a God he couldn't wait to meet and learn from.

'There is a God, and the Spirit of God in the first verses, this means He, God was not alone'.

We are off to a good start.

'This is my first lesson, I do not have to feel alone, there are times when I have done so and although I know nothing as yet about the God of this book, if he wasn't alone does this mean I am not alone ever?

The God I now want to know has been with me all the time! Is He the person in this room all the time?

Yes I like it, I will never be alone'.

'What makes people lonely though?'

Daniel, can you not see?

It is very simple.

Self does!

Loneliness can be experienced in the heart of anyone; there is no special time for it to hit us. Whether in a crowd or on our own it can be there, loneliness brings its own brand of melancholy from the past and for our future it can create its own fear.

To understand loneliness we must understand where it comes from, and the negativity we yield to.

It is the voice saying, 'I am lonely, nobody loves me, and as my name is '**negativity**' I do not like being ignored'.

As we learn the rules to a moral life, and live them we are able to cope with the rules which surround loneliness, we must never nurture it, and to overcome is the rule.

If you understand something, you will face it with joy and gladness in your heart and there will be a natural healing through being positive and eventually the sad loneliness of the past will go and bring a joyful quietness of rest.

We will be at peace with the past.

Daniel looked at me, and from the look on his face it was plain to see he was silently saying 'we can leave this can't we and continue'!

There was an issue here to be healed.

Loneliness can bring sorrow.

He went on with, 'it is very easy to understand, in the beginning it was God who created the heavens and the earth'.

It didn't surprise me at the understanding Daniel was displaying. 'I wasn't born then of course, but I was conceived in the mind of God just as you were writer lady in the beginning, I became a purpose, and I became important to God'.

Everyone is important to God.

'I love it; at last I know someone cares for me.'

'Yes I do like it, I was created'. Daniel went on,

'Then we have, Let there be light, this is good, we have those very words, it is good, and it gets better, I have the light to enable me to read what more could I ask? There is an inner light for our understanding and an outer light for our work'.

'I believe, are you listening to me writer friend of mine?

I, Daniel can believe, I do believe in what I am reading

This book does have power and in the first three verses'.

He was saying, 'I believe the light for the world which is day, somehow goes with the written 'Word', they go together, I believe somewhere in here is the understanding of God in the natural world'.

'Understanding The Bible, although I haven't read very much as yet, I believe God must be the light Himself, I know there will be revelation I just have to read more and get things in the right order don't I?'

The question needed no answer.

Have you noticed Daniel was throwing out nick names, I have been given 'writer lady' and if he is happy and relaxed why would I argue?

'The God who created me seems to be all knowing somehow?'

To see Daniels face as he is relating the first sentences of The Bible gave me excitement.

How about you? Do you want him to hurry along to hear his next words?

After he shares each little snippet, a silence develops, and it is in this silence I see Daniel listening as if someone is quietly speaking to him telling him to heed what has just been read.

His face betrays many emotions then it clears, as if he received a message, a revelation of understanding to the written words he just read.

He knew he had to pour out completely everything; he wasn't to leave anything out.

Daniel continues, 'as I read on about the creation of the earth, I get such an excitement and I think I will explode'.

'I have noticed when telling you about my new food for this is what I feel I am receiving, the explosive build up within me just disperses with each word I utter, what I have learnt goes and as soon as I start reading again I get refilled.

'Do you understand?' he asked me.

Yes I do, and so will your readers.

Even though I knew what he was saying, I wondered if I had ever heard them from The Word like Daniel; it is a privilege to write about this journey not just to hear it, and to see how God of The Bible works on a heart which has no hesitation in believing.

A heart which belongs to a babe as yet and as Daniel gives out more and more information for his journey understanding comes, and this can only come from the words of his Bible.

Have people put so much of themselves in the words, they miss the point altogether?

Yes I believe they have.

Already, Daniel knows the face behind The Bible he hasn't seen it yet but he knows it just as he knows the voice, and his sharing has only just started, as 'in the beginning'.

Daniel came out with something which could be considered by some as religious.

Religiosity is something many of us when new believers experience, we become world experts on God, are we really so ignorant and arrogant?

Maybe

In the beginning yes we were, and as we change becoming fishers of men, as well as farmers, reaping a harvest to sow and feed the followers, and keep the sheep from scattering we will eventually have all the food we need and this is how we will have the arrogance and ignorance taken away leaving knowledge and humility.

It is a profound or divine mystery to why Daniel was given this insight. But he has all the acumen needed to deal with it.

He said 'It doesn't matter what anyone says to me about this book, or about the people, the most important issue is how I react to the words in it'.

Don't you love him?

It was very plain to Daniel, he was and is important to the God who created him, and this being so he knows full well he must return this love with respect for this is due.

Daniel also knew he was certainly never to put Him on a pedestal, with the understanding, if God is on a pedestal He would be unreachable to Daniel, you and me.

As you are reading this narrative you can believe you are just as important to God as Daniel and I are.

Daniel said, 'I must read the Bible with only one objective, to learn about The Word, and I must learn to retain every word I read forever'.

Whoa up here!

Is this necessary if you have read with a heart full of love and good intent, the very one who wants to enter into your everyday life, who wants to be with you for ever more will do all your remembering for you. *__John 14: 25-27__*

'This means I do not have to fill myself up with the words I read and swallow, and in the right time those very words, will be brought back to me'. He stared at me.

'I knew it would be easy for me, I knew it with an inner knowledge'.

Daniel asked. 'What do I say when I come out with something profound when I have a deep moment?'

It would be like medicine if you were able to see Daniel's face; it was brighter than I have ever seen it.

'You know I didn't like myself, I have just become aware of this. I didn't like who I was I see now, it was my attitude which made me the black sheep of the family'.

'Is there a word to say I understand?'

I replied 'Hallelujah' is 'Praise the Lord', and does just fine I will have to learn how to spell it won't I?

Sometimes he takes the very breath out of me!

There wasn't a doubt in my mind Daniel would 'Hallelujah' a lot more through this journey.

As we walked through the creation of animals and read about the giving of dominion over them to us, Daniel smiled for the first time spontaneously.

'What a good understanding to have, all the trees, fruit everything there is,' he said, and then his eyes just about fell out of his head, he was hit with the realization everything on this earth was Gods' alone no one actually owned anything'.

'Does this mean when I kick something I am kicking the God who created it?

When I abuse someone am I abusing God?'

Daniel was looking slightly aghast; his face had a sickly appearance to it. I know he was thinking about his past, and he had me doing the same, bringing the past into the present.

Another pill to swallow only this time the past couldn't hurt; it was the learning from it which came back.

I had to prod him to move on with the journey, and as he relaxed it was me who said 'Hallelujah'.

It was fun being with Daniel on his journey through God's creation of Adam. Walking with someone who really is an innocent into the Spiritual realm, took me back to the first time I looked at the Bible with love and dread in my eyes.

Sometimes innocence is so wise.

Daniel said, 'God said 'let us make man in our image,' and he pointed out once again, 'I am not alone, I really love this saying'.

As man was created first from dust in His image, does God look like mankind? Is there a key here somewhere to the way we are created? I now see for the first time God doesn't say 'it is good'.

'Women are brought into the scene'.

'The creation of the first woman, women were molded by the Masters own hand'.

Then he asked, 'by the way what do we call the sentences I read out to you? They seem to hit me.'

I had to laugh for I actually noticed every now and then Daniel physically moved his head quickly to the left.

They are called 'scriptures' if you read them as they are written in the Bible.

If you use your own words giving the same message, you can say you are using your own words, quoting from a scripture. ***Revelations 22: 18-21***

Don't use the written word to mislead, for this is not acceptable to God, when quoting the meaning it must line up with what The Word says.

'That is good', said Daniel and laughed out loud, for he heard himself quoting from 'The Word'.

I do not know about you, but Daniel has a way of creeping into your heart, it seems impossible to feel anything other than love for him.

'I am not too sure about this next chapter', he said, 'where the serpent comes and the fruit gets a bite taken out of it.

As I see it, who told who to eat it, Adam or Eve is not the full extent of the,' a grin came upon the face in front of me, 'scripture the fact is a sneaky serpent decided it was time to put a spanner in the works of God'.

Daniel said, out of nowhere, 'so my life has been in the hands of a snake up until now?'

'Why has this changed? And how is it I can now clearly see there is a better way to live, without a serpent ruling me although I remember you told me to stay alert in case the serpent hisses.

What is happening, and where do I go from here?'

Now is the time

It is time to ask the three 'w 'questions what, where, why, who, when, questions, otherwise our journey is going to be of naught use to any of us.

Daniel **_what_** do you want from reading this book? What do you want from reading the Bible? 'I want true knowledge of The Word, and knowledge of how The Word wants me to live from now on. I want to be able to understand with my inner self the Bible'.

Where do you want to go with your knowledge Daniel?

'I want to go out and see everyone gets the opportunity to read about the creator of the World'.

Why?

'Well in the first few lines of reading The Bible I found a peace just came over me, there was no explainable reason for this, I also realized there was a hunger in me to keep on reading. I know I will always have this hunger reading the Bible will never be enough.

The **why** is within me, there is really no other reason?

Before you ask me the next question, I have to know **who** this person is who wants me to change; I know it is so important for reading The Bible, and if full understanding is to be the main purpose, and finishing the why question, I want to be a new person'.

When?

'Right now! The knowledge I have is in my head it seems to be on the outside of me, and I am not going to get any nearer to the real person who orchestrated my life at creation; **He** is now with me yes **He** is not with me as yet in the fullness I want. I have the chance now to become who I was made to be. And it is going to be fun finding out who I am'.

Hallelujah.

SPRING
Daniels Enters into his Third Season
New Growth and Glory

'Remember me'?

'I am Daniel trying to contain myself from rushing forward; well I like to think I am. There has been so much happening in my life, and the days are beautiful even when it's raining, and although I haven't changed my work place, there has been a change in my work'?

'My new position is now the foreman, yes, this looks good on paper, and yes before you ask I do get more money in my pay packet'.

'For the casual observer, nothing has really changed because the change is on the inside, it is in my heart.

'Breaking the bondage of man has given me freedom from the clutches of the Devil, and through reading the Bible daily has me growing in 'The Word' and my progress and acceptance of the author has covered me I am protected.

It is not the Bible doing the protecting for in reality it is a book, a beautiful one but only a book.

What was needed for understanding was the protection from the Author 'The Word' Himself', and as soon as I knew this I couldn't relinquish myself fast enough to Him.

I had to find out how this could happen for I only knew a little about the 'whys and wherefores' of The Word, I learnt about the Cross and all it stands for and with the certainty of my release, my entire self was to receive full understanding needed at the time, and this knowledge I am 'guarding jealously' I am going to keep it safely within me, for it is through my spiritual knowledge my spiritual food comes to me.

'There is an inner peace in everything I do and wherever I go I see beauty, I no longer am tongue tied unable to find words to describe how I feel or see things, and when I am asked to describe something I have new eyes to look it, and my descriptions are fuller they have the minute detail only the creator can give to us'.

'I still go for my walks I really enjoy the air of freedom around me. Each time I answer invitations to meals with my work colleague's families. May you see I have become a social person, and what is surprising I am enjoying myself'.

The peace surrounding me now is growing stronger, since my first touching The Bible this peace has never left me; in fact there are times when it has me like a deer in his wallow. It is like eating marshmallows, so soft and tasty.

'I feel so contented and as I continue everyday to read scriptures from the many chapters of my very precious book, I meet with new people from within the pages.

There are all manner of people in it, just like here on earth some have done tremendous works, and some have made tremendous mistakes'. Even Kings have made mistakes.

Whoever they are, I have a new understanding about God, yes I have met Him, and through the pages he reveals Himself to me, I see there is still plenty of reading ahead for me if I am to know Him as He wants me to here on earth, and to know Him totally, I will have to wait until His second coming.

It was said this was going to be, so I know for sure because it has been said, it will happen'.

'I am in the place where I know from an inner recognition The Word is God.

How do I know this, just listening to my heart and reading the Bible'?

Daniel has changed.

Anyone who knew him a few months ago would be surprised at the change of this once dour person he has become a very adaptable lovable man.

There are many who do not give an iota about any the change if they see it, for Daniel will just be Daniel, to them whatever.

They accepted him as he was and as far as it goes, that is how he is.

Daniel is always ready with an anecdote now on both his past, and the present, like now as he talks to me.

'It is so very exciting for me, and this bit I must share for it really made me laugh, my work mates wanted to know what kind of pep pills I was taking, I said without hesitation 'words from The Bible'.

'Sometimes what we say can turn around and bite us as happened not to me, but to my workmates. The three men are married with children, and at work considered to be rough diamonds, and I mean really rough'.

'They found a Bible one day and were sniggering together about it; at first they were not too bothered that I saw them doing this, for initially they had planned to play a joke on me for reading it'.

'It backfired for the one who took it home to plan the attack found he was reading it; I am talking here about The Bible, and he liked what he read'.

'The initial reason went out the door and all of these rough diamonds over a period of a few weeks found they were sharing what they read with one another, and then yes with me'.

It was obvious we didn't understand what the book was saying, and then suddenly one day something snapped within us all, and we became what we thought fluent in the word'.

'One minute we knew nothing and the next we knew everything!

We become Bible bangers, the experts.

Since sharing this episode with others I have been told this is spiritually natural, with natural man, a part of the introduction in a walk with God'.

There is always someone who likes to be the expert!

It has to be understood it is part and parcel of the natural and spiritual war we go through, it is to help us see once again the choice factor, and we learn these two will never abide together in harmony.

For natural man, and spiritual man will never be friends.

Daniel said 'It was over the first chapter of Genesis we became the experts'.

'There is so much to learn and the deep calls the deep. ***Psalm 42:7***

We eventually came to realize in this life time we were never going to know it all'.

'Looking at the words on the surface there was no message, so we let ourselves be lead into some understanding of what we were being told by the written word, through this we learnt how to understand a little more of the message, only the surface messages though'.

'There was no doubt at all we were going to find out from our continued reading together, there were five of us, with the wives and children joining in sometimes and as we slowly heeded what was written we were able to have good detailed discussions'.

'Everything was the real truth we did see this as fact, and it was right for us to be together, but it made the discussions show us we were getting nowhere'.

More so once we agreed with what we read, to have more than one reading together was right for we knew there was someone with us. ***Matthew 18: 19***

If the Bible agreed with us we knew we must be right.

Heaven and Earth, as in the Lord's prayer. ***Matthew 6; 9-13***

There is a purpose in all we do'.

I must in all truth say here not one of us knew what our purpose was, we believed we were going to find it somewhere between these covers'.

We knew we had a tutor with us, but not one of us laid claim to the title.

There were so many issues arising from reading The Bible and they were from inside each one of us. We seemed unable to talk to anyone else about our group what we were about, we never started a conversation off about the Bible, and when someone asked what we were up to, we would laugh it off 'nothing really, just a book club'.

'It was as if we had a secret to keep from others, it could be said we were embarrassed by our new style of life'.

'Were we selfishly holding on to something we didn't want to share, or rather was it we didn't want to be ridiculed about it, the latter was more likely nearer to the truth'?

'One of the wives said we had to find out more about this book, why it was out there with the public, why it was number one seller in the world.

On this we all agreed, for each one of us knew the word secret in anything could mean occultism or some such thing'.

'Our question was how would this be, when we were reading the Bible? Does it lead to occultism?'

Yes it can do if there is no understanding and the focus is on you other than the real God.

Daniel told me how they broke from going nowhere to going somewhere, and then it came from a kindly man who was a respected, and well loved retired Pastor.

'Listen to this, his name was Moses Truelove, and he had been a Pastor for many years, one who never went to a Theologian College; he said all his training was from his experiences and through the Voice and Hand of God.

His preference of name is and always will be Brother Moses, and he calls me Brother Daniel. It is the brotherhood in Christ which brought us together, it was our hunger and his understanding of the Word.

His conviction was so strong we could feel the pull of it, and this was enough to have us on bended knee.

We were told, 'in this day and age, there is a sad loss to the understanding of the 'Word of God' in our Bible, and to get this we must start with 'Jesus'.

We must learn who true love is. And this is not our new friend although he came to us in love for his brothers and sisters in Christ; for that is what he did.

Our new friend came to share with us each evening and through him we were introduced to true love, Jesus. We met with Jesus and through Him we about turned from what started off as looking impossible, into living a life of the easiest and most beautiful lifestyle on earth.

We continued reading and discussing the Word from Matthew in the New Testament, and followed Jesus through his early life'.

Daniel asked me one day when having a much needed break from our writing,

'You knew I had to know Jesus first didn't you?

Then, 'Have you notice that Jesus was a carpenter?'

Well no, to the first and yes, to the second question.

I know we can't go anywhere positively without Jesus, but remember Daniel this is your journey, and you are telling everyone your experiences, how you came to find the Bible and how you came to know the Holy Spirit, and be a help to others.

Do you know you have a Spirit, do you know who I am speaking about, or is this to come?

I was looking for some reaction from Daniel we all have a Spirit.

It is our spirit which will recognize the Spirit of God, and this is how I live with the Spirit of God residing within me, I see all there is around me through my Spirit, not as the flesh sees, but as the Word sees. ***Luke 10: 23-24***

This sets one apart from the earthly realm.

Two worlds and one Spirit through our own repentance.

We can stand in the gap for those who need to pick up their own cross. The gap is the distance between the way things are and how they should be.

From his look of surprise I knew he believed in Jesus, he believed in the words of the Bible he knew the Holy Spirit, but had not made the commitment to believe on the Word written about in the Bible and there is a difference. If we believe on Jesus we will act like Him and do what He said we could and would do, such as bigger and better things.

I knew Daniel was getting closer to walking on the path of righteousness as were his fellowship brothers and sisters.

Getting to know Jesus is beautiful, and just as those who get to know Him become beautiful within.

Daniel was making progress.

There are some very big choices to be made, our surrender to another control must be 100%, if that doesn't happen then we will be going one step forward and two steps backward each day.

Our decision to make this choice can be for some very difficult, for the control we are relinquishing to is invisible, and to do this in bold confidence we must know God, we must know the Word of God. We must want His control over our lives, nothing is more positive than to live within the control of our heavenly Father in Heaven.

We continued with our work and Daniel continued learning about the God who created him, the God who came to earth as man, and through his learning it was possible to gather knowledge with an understanding what life can be without guilt, pride, shame, rebellion, hatred.

We have arrived at the day when Daniel said to me 'I would like you to listen to my revelation about 'light'; and it was the way he said light that filled with me intrepidness. I prayed for courage to hear what he was going to say, I was filled with anticipation, are we there, had the time arrived for Daniel to say he had relinquished his life to the cause of Christ?

Did he want to commit his life to emulate Jesus?

'Well,' he started.

Don't you love it when someone starts off like that?

Not!

'Do you remember when I said God my Creator could be the light?' ***Ephesians 5: 8-14***

'Well I now know Jesus is certainly the light He has said so Himself, ***John 8:12,*** and what is more my fellowships brothers and sisters, now have this understanding, to live we must walk in His light. Sounds crazy I know but this whole journey is somewhat beautifully crazy don't you think'?

'We have been studying the New Testament, and why Jesus came to earth, we know a commitment to this cause is needed from each one of us, not as a fellowship it has to be as an individual, we are floating around in limbo although we moved from the negative, to the positive way of thinking.

What we need to do is go to our Master in humble repentance for this is the way to receive total forgiveness from Him.

The removal of our past sins is to humble oneself in total forgiveness knowing full well and admitting out loud we have lived in sin, there must be recognition of our own selfish nature, and when we do this we will have completed the needed guidelines to live a life of peace for ever more.

What I am saying is our life although the same won't be trampled on, unless we let it, by the creatures in the control of our **enemy**'. *Luke 10: 19*

Well, well, don't you just love someone, who has the hand of God on them?

The vendetta, the misunderstandings we get, must have light thrown upon them. Daniel and his little fellowship's mind sets have to be cleared up and brought into line with the Word. Wrong thinking is deception and a tool of the deceiver.

Clarity in our thinking is important we must be scripturally correct so as not to mislead others we are to walk as the scripture suggests.

'This is the way walk ye in it' *Isaiah 30:21*

We are to walk in the truth and so be able to stand up before the Word of God and say 'I believe'. Meaning what we say must be from the depths of our hearts. And if it agrees with the word of God He will see it does not return to us void.

We cannot display any false humility we are to be lowly of heart like Jesus Himself, if we are carrying prideful humility and know it we are in sin. The scripture *Numbers 32: 23-24* says emphatically that your sin will be found out. Anything we hide will be uncovered. *Luke 16: 17.*

A scripture can change the hearts and minds of any travellers on this journey; for in the beginning we thought we knew everything. Huh?

Ephesians 6:12. You may have heard this scripture; and it is the full comprehension of it, we need to grasp.

So many Christians never look at themselves when something goes wrong they will blame others every time. *Ephesians5:6-17* this may well be others have contributed to a situation letting it grow out of proportion, and this point may be fact.

In truth Christians do not fight against a brother or sister if we are doing so we are pleasing the enemy of God.

We have been deceived by God's enemy so our fighting becomes sinful, there is really only one way to deal with all our problems and there is a correct procedure in the Bible for us to follow bringing us back into living the truth.

Matthew 18:15-20, 1Corinthians 6: 1-8a

Wars in families usually start through a negative attitude.

Daniel already knows this as fact.

We only have **one enemy** in this world.

The enemy of God!

This is whether you are a Christian or not.

To give the enemy a title, Deceiver, Devil, Satan, Lucifer, and he has many, many more; he hides and lives in the cover of darkness.

Luke 8: 16-18.

We have one more season to journey through and in it Daniel for the first time from the very depths of his heart reveals now the urgent desire from those many years ago, as he takes us through to the end of his story sharing with us what he has learnt, a mantle of gentle persuasion picks him up, and carries him along as a gentle river takes the flow of crisp clean water to another destination.

If we too want this we can come into a life of contentment and understanding of the 'Word' from the Bible.

He shares with us fellow travelers, and it is through Daniel's very own understanding of The Word, we the readers are seeing the Lord Himself.

SUMMER THE FOURTH SEASON
As all darkness slowly ebbs away,
The final step on the journey begins where
Daniel knows only Truth can prevail.

We have had a break from one another and in some ways this has been a lesson in itself, if not for Daniel it was for me. I often wondered what Daniel was up to, if he was going forward or backward, 'ye of little faith' ***Matthew 6:30-34,*** were the words which came to me the day he bounced into the office brighter than a sunbeam.

It was obvious Daniel was bursting at the seams ready to spill all the happenings of his new life onto the screen.

His confidence was oozing and spreading all over me; I have never doubted Christ from the day I gave my life to Him, and now, I see this same confidence is going to strengthen as Daniel and I finish his journey.

The new man in front of me had a permanent smile.

'I have had', Daniel said, 'the most illuminating few weeks; you will never believe what has happened and who has been the most critical of me'.

Laughter was in the air, it was contagious for laugh we did, and for the first time in harmony, at last we were both in tune.

Before we each had our own joke, we were on opposite sides of the fence, and right now even though we both knew the issues to follow are serious our understanding of them was through our faith.

We had to agree on what we were going to write and in doing so Daniels readers would be able to have understanding through their own faith and the words would give out inner food.

Matthew 18:19-20

I said to Daniel I have been where you are, please remember this for it is through my own experiences, I am able to recognize where you are coming from, our journey has always been on the same path, who we know out there, waving my hand towards the window, is the only difference between us.

Now Daniel continues ending his own story.

'You will remember the pastor friend of ours', Daniel sighed then spilt out, 'he comes to share every day, he has become a real brother, and we were suspicious at first and wondered at the amount of time he spent with us.

I see now all who go through the transition of flesh to Spirit are of the mind, they are the only people to do so.

'We asked him why us?

All he said was 'why not you, I pray I will see you young ones grow into, The Bible'.

'Isn't this beautiful, it is beautiful to know there is something beyond. There are those who really care for others and their walk in life is an encouragement'.

'Through our Brother Moses speaking as the mouth of Jesus; we became fourteen new creations, living in two worlds with only one Spirit, a Spirit which gives understanding to a new life.

How did this come about?'

Our Daniel certainly had been reaping a harvest to share with us. Through my discernment it was obvious although he was looking peaceful; there was something or someone trying to hold him down.

Daniel seemed excited, and withdrawn at the same time. On closer scrutiny it was obvious he had 'been got at', I could see a bruised reed. *__Isaiah 42: 3__*

There will be no wine today; poor sweet Daniel has hit the world of sour grapes! *__Ecclesiasticus 9:10. Apocrypha__*

There are many who consider they know God, they say they know all about Jesus.

Are they being really truthful, do they really know the Christ?

Do they follow everything He has said, or do they only follow Him to the point of what would be considered by a true follower nothing other than looking out for self, with a convenient God?

Does your heart bleed for him?

Daniel has touched on something many true believers know in their heart to be fact, as well as truth.

'People have no problem hiding behind the cover of God, in reality they are the people who tell you to go to church, they are the people who have become religious in there own traditions. They believe they have the right to call you into line and by what'?

'It is only through their criticism of you!

They believe they have the right to become your judge and jury'. *Matthew 7:1*

Daniel as well as his fellowship members of young learners, in the school of Christ, found out from the land of hard knocks nothing is as easy as living in the past.

Although the burdens of their pasts had not allowed them to go forward, they had never seen the competitiveness they were seeing clearly now from the hearts of believers, the whole outcome of their lives had changed completely.

'Roundabout turns, being reborn, beginning again, only this time in God's way.

The lessons on Christian behaviour have begun, and from the beginning of our initial journey, we are now on a journey within it, the Word of God from the Bible has brought Daniel out of Egypt with Moses.

With an inner strength helping him, Daniel has thrown down a dragnet, and we are being drawn out of our Egypt with him, where we have been in bondage to our past.

'As we continue our journey, the God of Love is revealed and you will want to open your own hearts to receive Him.

A painter would know there are many shades of grey not just light or dark grey, this is where it stops though, for as a follower of Christ we like Daniel know grey is not in the kaleidoscope of colours, we have in the rainbow, also the Word of God is white. There is no black, or grey, there is no neutral ground for this would mean we are going nowhere, think about it if a car is in neutral out of gear we could slide, we must be in gear to go anywhere with purpose, right or wrong it is choices again isn't it?

There are no in betweens, the Word is pure truth white as snow, deceit is from the devil and immorality lives in darkness which is black'.

Daniel had so wanted to understand this and it came to him the day Brother Moses said we can only understand the Word of God from the Bible through the Son of God and the reason is so simple for the 'Word' is Jesus.

Jesus wants to teach us the Bible Himself; He wants to lead us himself through repentance into becoming sinless, so we can enter the Kingdom of Heaven.

We can have this learning with or without pain. In this life with Jesus, or in the next life which will be painful.

All will be taught by God. ***John 6:45***

Jesus must reside in our hearts as a resident and then the Spirit will at the appropriate time, reveal all the secrets. ***Daniel 2:29, 2:47, Amos 3: 7.***

From the Old Testament and from The New Testament we are told Jesus wants to teach us and if we obey we will be lead into repentance.

As Jesus is no longer with us as a person ***John 15: 26,*** it is His Spirit which will teach us. ***John 14: 26*** He is alive within our hearts.

Our brain which is sometimes called our grey matter is completely bypassed and without surgery, if we read and understand with the mind we will no doubt have analyzed the word through our natural human thinking.

Missing the purpose of a message which if searching for no doubt was needed.

This need is a spiritual need not a physical need.

We are going to look closely at the allegory of Daniels journey, and if we bring it together with our own lives on the journey we will see how important it is to know Jesus if we want to understand the total Bible, and live within its boundary of morality.

Father God is our main source of food, God is the root of our very passion for wanting to live a sinless life, and every person needs to know this.

Along the way we are being led to learn about the men and women, who will bring us closer to this main source.

We can liken our journey to an overseas experience.

When we travel to a new country, we land at an airport, and from then on until we leave this country we are in new territory.

We go to a travel brochure, and search out the sights we want to see still within the overall country which is the mainstay; it is the foundation the stronghold.

As we travel on these trips within the country, we are learning about new people, and their natural way of living.

On the journey Daniel is taking us we have God as the main country, and Jesus as the travel brochure, only difference is we are travelling through a book, within a book and always after each visitation with new people, we come back to the living waters of God who is our main stay, who is our food and we are sustained for the next visit.

We are learning a new way of life, and the country is a Spiritual one.

Listening and obeying. There is a very fine line with Christian obedience and within this fine margin we will learn the way to live in peace, which the world does not know as yet.

We read about David bringing the Ark of the Covenant to the city of Jerusalem ***2 Samuel 6.*** There were a few hiccups and it actually didn't make it at first.

Only the priests were allowed to touch the ark. This was an order from above and when the oxen stumbled, Uzzah put out his hand and touched what was forbidden, in doing so he encountered the wrath of God, and for this irreverent act God struck him down.

It is all about obedience; disobedience is a sin, with the wages of sin being death.

Romans 6:23, Romans 2:11-16

Daniel has become so dear to us and we see those who have come in contact with him have been drawn like a magnet, not who he is, they are drawn for what he now has, it is so obvious to everyone who knew him, his whole personality has changed.

He has become a very lovable person, and he finds it impossible to do anything other than love fellow mankind.

It is with this love he continues to unravel the last threads of doubt and misconception which has had him sitting on the top of a fence, just waiting to jump into the clean air with a clean heart.

He use to take quiet offence at what people said, now his heart no longer is offended, instead of defending him self with an attitude of silence, he attacks his ill feeling with inner strength and becomes an overcomer in the Lord.

Daniel continues, 'What Brother Moses did for me and our little fellowship was what the Prophet Moses in Numbers of the Bible did for the Israelites;

He showed them the escape from Egypt was so necessary and why we must throw off the same chains of slavery, for those chains are the chains of the bondage we unknowingly carry. Bondage is oppressive it is from the devil and it holds us down getting heavier as each moment passes. Our spine becomes bent and so we walk bent over instead of upright and tall. The sins we carry are a burden to be rid of as soon as possible, better now than never. 'It is our physical work we like to talk about, working too hard is physical bondage, which bends us over.

Who is holding the gun to your head, you are yourself with the devil saying to you, 'You must do this and you must do that!'

Is Satan tempting you to be foolproof? Yes he is!

About the tempting of Jesus, the devil tried to trap Him after he was baptized, the relevance here it was after his baptism, the Bible says it happened so we must heed and see why and what we are being told.

Was a sinless man Jesus coming out of his own Egypt?

Jesus stayed pure until his horrendous death and then at such time he would, yes he would take all our sins and all the sins of the world.

This was done at the Cross on the hill at Calvary. Not one sinful thing was missed. At that time Satan was defeated. ***Matthew 4: 1-11***

What happened to Jesus in the wilderness was no other than Satan tempting Him with our sins; these are the same sins mankind can carry and all from the fall of Adam.

The carrying of them kept the Israelites in slavery, eventually leading to their exodus experience from Egypt?

Jesus was tempted by the devil for forty days and forty nights, and never once did He yield to the wily whims of the crafty serpent.

The serpent already knew with the coming of Jesus he was defeated, he kept on trying though for why would Herod try to destroy the baby and why was it said 'no good thing came out of Nazareth'.

It was after the wilderness temptation Jesus began to preach. ***Matthew 3: 13-17***

He was totally clean having never sinned himself from his birth to his death. Of course at his death he took upon himself all *our sins* so we would have a channel to God through His blood and ask forgiveness and repent becoming over comers as we are to be, through His name as well.

This shows us we must speak the Word with the authority, given through the blood and name of Jesus we must be of clean heart.

We read about Noah who built an Ark in ***Genesis 6,*** and in ***Genesis 7: 17*** we read 'for forty days the flood kept coming on the earth, we see once again a cleansing this time of the whole world'.

'In some ways I think of the waste then I see the treasure we have been given, Adam and Eve had to fall into sin, Jesus had to come to earth as man, and of course you wouldn't be here nor would I in a sinful state. There has been emphasis on the love of Christ and Jesus has shown us the way to choose.

For he didn't come to praise the devil who incidentally was thrown out of heaven as a fallen angel, Jesus came to destroy the works of the devil.

Revelations 12:7-9, Isaiah 14:11-15.

'Jesus came to give us backbone; he came to overcome all evil. What a waste it would have been if we hadn't lived on earth, and found out there is way to live our lives without the hassles of lies and deceit, and what a waste it would be if we didn't know it was Jesus who is the treasure who walked the earth as man, and what a waste it would be if we didn't realize he has seen us at our worst, and what a waste if we didn't know it is his footsteps we are to walk in doing bigger and better things waiting for the second coming.

He is going to come again, we do not know when, why should we? When he does we shall be like Him.

1 John 3: 1-3.

We know we are to be clean as Jesus stayed while walking through the temptation of the devil'.

Here Daniel stared at me then said, 'we, I know are to be imitators of Jesus Christ Himself'. As Daniel was speaking it made me think back to when I started my new life with Christ and I remembered the feelings I had within myself. There was an excitement as well as an emptiness as all past bondage was removed, it left a gap like I was gutless not in the sense of having no fight in me this has always been there, no it was like having no nourishing food. There was a gap waiting for food. The food of God comes from His own Word.

Daniel heard my thoughts for he picked up straight away about food, and off we went on the journey again.

'In the beginning we read where there is freedom to eat from any tree in the Garden of Eden *Genesis 2:15-17*. There was small print though the 'don'ts' and this was not to eat from the tree of knowledge of good and evil, for when you eat of it you will surely die.

'With the results Eve listened to the serpent, offered the fruit to the devil in Adam, and we have our first glimpse of hell'.

'This is the fall of mankind; anyone born from then on will be born into a natural world full of sin.

Man will have to labour from this time on for his food, and women will have labour pains at childbirth and the serpent will slither along on his belly'. ***Genesis 3: 14***

'Food why do we need it, to restore our bodies, and whatever for when we actually abuse it'? This is an interesting way of looking at our food intake.

Daniel went on, 'Moses on the exodus from Egypt had food problems with the oppressed Israelites, Moses was commanded to speak to the rock ***Numbers 20: 8*** then in his anger against the people for they were moaning and groaning he raised his arm and struck the rock twice with his staff. ***Numbers 20: 9-11.*** Then as I read on I saw how careful we have to be, obedience and trust. They go together'.

'Speak means open your mouth to utter sounds, also at this time it would have been better if Moses wasn't angry'. 'As I continued reading in ***Numbers 20: 12.*** Moses was denied the privilege of taking the Israelites into the Promised Land. This is a tremendous lesson for me, as I was reading the Bible I saw again the intervention of God's power and His miracles, without faithful trust in Him yes I too could be denied the privilege of Him working through me to do an important work.

What do you think about all of this Writer Lady?'

Help! Where is all this coming from where is Daniel getting his understanding and revelations?

What a book the Bible is!

There is only one answer, through God, through The Word, written in the Bible!

Smiling quietly Daniel said, 'As I have been learning from the Word of God with the mentoring of Brother Moses I have heard myself, many times come out with statements and my Brother says 'thank you for feeding me as well'.

One of these revelations was when reading about King David and his life. David started off with the killing of the giant Goliath as a young boy, and later he was to become a great king.

'He like Moses made a mistake in his life with not going to fight a battle staying home instead, all of this made good reading, it is easy to see how the devil likes to interfere in God's work.

A king would lead his army into battle, and David as king should have been with his army every time it went to fight. Once though he stayed in Jerusalem on other important business well he thought so anyway.*2 Samuel 11.*

I pondered over this very story, and David knew right from wrong and as the king he should have led his men into the battle.

All the bad things which followed his staying at home murder and immorality are signs only of the devil, there is also another way to look at it, and this is the fact David was disobedient. I have learnt when I go into battle I am going with a king and an army, and they are right in front of me as well as behind me, I am protected totally.

The scriptures says I am not to be discourage at those who are against me I know they will be a vast army*, 2 Chronicles 20: 15*

I must pick up another scripture and remember, who is in front of me and who is my rear guard*. Isaiah 52: 15*

We are going forward, moving on through the Old Testament and as we do so we are gathering momentum, our understanding is coming to the fore, and what we have picked up and taken on board ourselves all started at the creation 'in the beginning' with the Word.

We have Adam pure as fresh snow, then Eve, the fruit and we have the wily serpent, who brought along his witchcraft and other sins which follow the devil, on the positive side we have the knowledge of obedience to God, we know faith, our belief which are the same, and trust are our stepping stones with Him.

Our trust is in God and on The Word. We have learnt from the Old Testament David was taught by God himself, and the words were as sweet as honey in his mouth.

What have we learnt from the New Testament?

The Rock, we stand upon is Jesus and it is this very rock which Moses struck *1 __Corinthians 10:4__* he struck what was holy, and it got worst he did so in front of those he was leading.

In everything we do we must do so for the Glory of God.

Who wants their own words to come back and bite them?'

Once we have uttered something whether for or against someone the words can never be retracted whether we have said them to people or to ourselves. Fact and truth!

Daniel has been blessed for he has taken the step to share his conversion with us and he has shared the telling of it with believing believers.

He already knows they love their walk with Christ, and will allow what is to be to happen, and will rebuke quietly, with an explanation the reason what is not to be.

'See the reasons are all written in the Bible they show us we must be like Jesus to walk in His footsteps.

First we were created the Bible says 'in his very own image' God's very own image which can be seen in Jesus Christ. Jesus has said if you have seen me you have seen the Father.

Jesus is the image of our invisible God, and we all go through a process to be like Him for whom else would we want to be like?

__2 Corinthians 3:18, Colossians 1: 15__.

We can never be Godly like God, but we can be like Jesus, who is part of the Godhead, he was there at our creation. Believe me the Bible says so. I was told it like this, one egg is made up of shell, yolk and white, the shell holds these together. It is God who holds Jesus and the Holy Spirit together. There is One God.

To be like Jesus we must allow God to work within us.

The Spirit of God will testify to our spirit we are God's children.

Not only His children, we are his friends this is quite humbling isn't it? *__John 15:15__*

Children, friends, we can call God 'Daddy' 'Abba', 'Father', we are brothers and sisters to Jesus, the Bible says he is not ashamed to call us brothers, *__Hebrews 2:11__*

God will provide all our needs and he loves us.'

'Being brothers or sisters [mankind] of Jesus is a privilege and there is no animosity at all, just good unconditional love for mankind.

We are just as pure as He Himself is in His eyes.

'There is no way we can bypass where the elements of distrust and jealousy come from to mankind, it all started at the fall of Adam, going to his two sons Cain and Abel, God looked with favour on Abel not on Cain so we have murder, a commandment not to break. Cain was the child of Satan'.

'We now have the father of all nations who was a man of God, his name is Abraham.

What a beautiful calling he had on his life,

__Genesis 12: 1-3__ a calling he picked up and walked with never looking back, and talking about looking back he took Lot with him. Lots wife looked back. Turning back is what she did thus turned into a pillar of salt. I read all about Lots family not a story I enjoyed although it is there and there certainly is a message in it.

Sexual appetites and the like can destroy us, as this family found out. Lot was a man who knew right from wrong and chose to live both'.

Genesis 19:26

'We have said we can never retract the words we utter whether they are in anger which is negative, or in love which is positive.

Abraham was the father of both Ishmael and yes Isaac. Same father with different mothers, step brothers. There is a start to another journey here.

From the moment Isaac was born there was adversity and from Ishmael's death onward his descendants would live in hostility towards all their brothers. ***Genesis 25:18.*** This is in rebellion against God of the Bible.

Isaac was the father of the twins Esau who was born first and Jacob. ***Genesis 25: 19-34***

With all the evil lying and cheating which went on with these two it is very obvious the devil was within their midst'.

'Brotherhood did have a nasty taste for the element of jealousy had entered within hearts. Coveting what another has, another commandment not to break. I told you I do not like coveting what we do not need.

Jacob made a coat of many colours for his second youngest son Joseph, and once again we can see the disharmony this action caused for his own brothers planned to destroy Joseph, the plans of men do not work out if God has blessed someone and we have an interesting story through the life of Joseph a boy of seventeen whom God showed the dreams of others for interpretation'.

'Now we come to Moses whom we have already mentioned, the commandments were given to Him from God to be written down, and it was he who delivered the Israelites from Egypt these were but a few of the tasks set before him.

Because of his anger he did not deliver the people in to the Promised Land this task was given to Joshua, the land given to him is where this courageous warrior is buried'.

God was with him all the time and kept on encouraging him to keep going forward.

This is the same with us God will give us all the encouragement we need to keep looking up'.

We are called the same way as Samuel was called, by God, when our name is called out we may hear it, ignore it or we may answer the call either way though we are going to be called in to the realms of the Spirit'. ***1 Samuel 3***

Samuel was the child of Hannah whom she promised to give to God, she honoured the promise and Samuel grew up in the temple with Eli the priest.

The off side to most of these stories is there. Time after time I see people wanting to be on the top side of the coin, the head, and they always want to be there yesterday, the Bible said, 'it is not by our works it is by the Spirit of God' and knowing that brings contentment to me'. ***Zechariah 4: 6*** 'There is an old adage 'pride before a fall' I have been there a few times on this journey to be sure and no doubt you have as well.

Now is the time to learn the difference between the Word and the scriptures.

'It is just so beautiful to belong to someone in reality at last for although Jesus is unseen, there is no doubt in my heart I belong to Him the same as all the other believing believers around me and there are many.

How do I belong to Jesus?

It happened because of The Word, I didn't have it explained to me it just happened'.

'As I continued with my studies of both the New Testament and the Old it was obvious they must be together, and as we have seen all the way through if we do not have a comparison there is no way we are going to be able to read the scriptures with the purpose of unravelling what we are being told to find.

The Bible is the recorded letters of prophets and saints, as well as the recorded words of Jesus when He was on earth. The saints from the Old Testament who followed God knew Him through faith'. ***Hebrew 11***

'They are the prophets Abraham, Noah, David, Moses, and others of that time.

What I had to learn and what I want to share with you is the uncovering of the bondage about the Bible which binds us to the deception of Satan.

We are going to break forth from Satan's binding link in the chain of bondage, and become free from the lies which have had us believing untruths'.

'Christianity believes the Bible is the '**Word** of **God**' and all the commands referring to the 'Word of God' Christians believe are referring to the Bible commands.

When in reality we are being told to go to God ourselves directly, and listen to the 'Word of God' the 'Voice of God' speaking to us'.

'My Sheep hear my voice and I know them, and they follow me'. *John 10: 27*

'If we are unable to listen to the Voice of God, we are never going to grow, never going to repent and we will never know the mercy and grace being offered to us, and further more we will be unable to find the true God.

This being so we can say in truth there will be no reward for us in the Kingdom of Heaven, or with Christ. Those who have spent weeks or years learning the Bible off by heart enabling them to quote any scripture at any time will gain nothing at all with God.

Has anyone looked to see when the first Bible was printed (1516) and then wondered what was used before that time?

Looking at this fact and truth, we can see it is our listening and obeying God's voice which brings about a change in us. We can see it is the Word of God that changes our lives.

How do we hear God's voice, is it so simple? Why aren't we doing just that?

And then the realization, Jesus had said 'it is the hungry and the thirsty who are God's chosen people'.

It is now printed indelibly upon my heart the fact; the Bible which is the book we are unravelling is not the, Word of God.

This makes one think doesn't it? Go back for a moment.

Satan has an army of carnal Christians, and I was one of them until I found there was still a gap in my life.

As I wanted so much to become a born again Christian I stepped forward to an altar call believing it was the way to become one. This is what happened.

As soon as I had been prayed over I was told I could go and sit down again. I am sorry to say this is all that happened and I didn't feel a thing and not one word had been uttered by me. It was come here and now go, and sit down. I was called in to make up numbers.

Brother Moses had told me life would seem different straight away, for the Word of God is living and active.

As I had never uttered a word about my belief, or confessed my sins, or asked forgiveness confessing all out of my mouth, nothing new happened. I want you to know and believe that Jesus will teach you and show you how to change, for He is the light who enlightens all men. *__John 1:9__*

One cold day with only Brother Moses and two of my Work colleagues as witnesses I told God from my heart I would dedicate my life to His service and make a commitment to serve Him from this day forward.

I confessed for I knew I was a sinner and I knew he was Jesus the Word resurrected.

It was then I was baptized in the river as did my witnesses. And was it exhausting, and as I came up out of the water covered with bright sunshine I felt a love which threw me into a state of weakness my legs did not belong to me. 'This is my Son and I am well pleased with him', were the words I heard from somewhere. Hallelujah.

I was the recipient of an anointing and by being quiet and focused, I could hear him, I could hear the living Word of God, I heard Christ.

We must remember everyone is and individual, and this may happen with the same results but the act may be different.

It is from Him we learn how to be cleansed, and as the cleansing happens we will know a surrender of mind, body and soul, and we will allow the leading of Him and then we will come to know what he wants us to know about Him. When the Word of God is within, we will be able to carry the Spirit of Truth.

Do not allow the devil to work in you, through you, do not allow him to chain you up, by saying you have done all you need to do. Just go and sit down.

'For it isn't right, we must surrender totally to the Holy Spirit. And we must confess to Him our love. We must commit ourselves to Jesus! And when we do so we will be able as time goes on to hear His voice and follow him'. ***John 10: 27***

There are many scriptures referring to the Word of God, and we usually interpret them as meaning the Bible, they are referring to the Voice of God, the Voice of the Lord.

The disciples were with Jesus, they walked with Him, listened to Him they learned from Him, they wrote letters yes, which are recorded in the Bible along with what Jesus said and taught them as well as His other followers. You and I.

Jesus was crucified, and came back with a task it was to see that the promised Spirit of Christ was received, the same spirit we receive when we accept Jesus and believe on Him and the blood of the lamb. With our verbal commitment of dedication to be a servant forever we are adopted into the family of Christ'. ***Revelations 7:14-17***

Writing Daniel's revelations has been an enjoyment one which has taken me to another level in my own walk with God, even though I have complete trust in the Lord and his Spirit and know he is the Word of God, ***John 1: 1-5*** I see how Daniel suffered along with the many others, I have done so myself.

Those who have come to know Jesus knowing him is a progression of growth with only one teacher and this has to be the 'Word Himself', and as the Word said 'come unto me, Take my yoke upon you, and learn of me, *Matthew 11: 28-29*

Daniel did just that with a driving hunger, and although he wanted more and more of the Word 'yesterday', it has to be in God's timing.

His grasp of the Bible has become thorough for he has never faltered in the belief Jesus is the Word. *1 John 2:27*

He has learnt the thoughts of God are not his thoughts, and also he knows not to follow his own brain, for he does not want to be gnashing his teeth in frustration and pain.

Daniel said 'There is new understanding of my life, there was some difficulty for me to find the narrow gate at first, I did get there and seeing the flip side of this, it would have been so much easier to go backward.

Going forward will keep me trim and able to seek God's face.

With an increasing glory I keep on heeding and obeying to stay where I am now. I know the journey with me will end when the last page is written; the most interesting thing is I know many who started on this journey of mine are now on their own seeking eternal life, and they know it will never end, unless they choose it to do so.

And if that does happen we would be backsliding, we would be walking away from God, and the most precious gift ever given to mankind. God Himself'.

'He gave each one of us a measure of himself. As we have already mentioned we are to be like Jesus, we are to be imitators of the Word of God.

We can if we allow Jesus through His Spirit to open up the secrets of the Bible for us and teach us all about Himself, the very God who frees us from sin which has the penalty of death, being free gives us eternal life and a lifelong Spirit to lead and guide us as we learn to love him, as he loves us'.

'The Bible has been blamed for so much over years gone by, and sad to say in many bookcases there is a dusty one waiting for a strangers hand to go out, and take it off the shelf.'

'Those many years ago when I dreamed of being a bearer of peace, and goodwill to man for the disharmony in the world, was such it tortured me; I had no understanding of the fact life is divided into two realms Spiritual and natural, and I could have started something and it may have avalanched taking me no doubt into a disaster zone through my ignorance'. Daniel knew it would have been wrong timing.

'All the anger and arguing I had with my family was for a purpose, and bitter as it was there was misunderstanding on both sides, with me I know it was the ignorance of youth, and as my parents were wanting the best for all their sons being a peace bearer, was ridiculous when there was a thriving furniture business waiting for me to step into'.

'It was the same for my great, great grandfather who had the same dream, to show others peace can exist if you look for it, even though he, and I didn't actually have it ourselves in the beginning.

What was wrong I know and keep on saying, for both of us our timing was not in tune with the 'One' neither of us knew, the one who controls everything in our lives.

The Word of God who was there in the very beginning of creation'.

'Unless we hear and see, there will certainly be no progress. God will not help the proud; he does help the humble though.

Jesus has said 'He, who has my words and keeps them, serves the Son. They will feel Christ and see the Way. And yes there is no doubt they will witness salvation. We are to remember the letter kills the Spirit gives eternal life.

The sacrifice of Jesus' life has been given to the few who would lose their own life to save it'.

'For my ancestor in his memory I can walk with zealous vigor toward what he wanted to do and what I am doing, I can do it because now I have a contact which neither of us had in the beginning, and our contact is Jesus, 'The Word'.

He is the first person in my life, and you listen carefully to this. He is not my shadow I am His, I follow Him. For I have died to self and am now hidden with Christ in God.

There are two candles one in each hand, both lit, both with bright flames, and as you bring one over to the other they become a bigger and brighter flame, two become one. ***Colossians 3: 2-4*** my flame is hidden in Christ the Word.

Having the knowledge of God through the Bible has led me into so many new situations and every one of them has been a blessing.

'I do not want to preach, I want to take the Word of God to the people I want to Evangelize in a big way, the Truth of God, it is in me, I am compelled to do so'. I want to let people see me as I am a child of the God most High, I want to let the people see me, the real me the one God loves and feeds daily, and know I do stand out, in the crowd.

'As we gathered around the saints from the scriptures whom we meet in the Bible, we learn from each one a new and wonderful way to serve God.

They all had something in their hearts to give whether it was big or small it was given spontaneously like the lady with her last coin, these people all gave not because they felt they had to, they gave because they wanted to please a God whom they loved.

This love drove them to give unselfishly to a God not for what he did for them; it was for who He was to them.

As we read for ourselves what God can do, we become more in awe of Him. Nothing is impossible to Him who loves us, and gave His own Son for us'. ***Luke 1: 37***

'Knowing God gives us an awesome fear of Him, and living within the power of the knowledge of this awe, we learn the truth about Him, we learn who He is, and no one else except God the Word of the Bible can be so totally faithful to His followers.

Knowing who I am in Christ has led me to knowing that I am nothing without Him, nothing at all. His Spirit leads me through all the situations needed for my growth and recovery from the realm I so readily followed never thinking it was anything other than right. Thinking this way was how my past behavior came over to others, and on reflection of my attitude I could become sad only I don't for I see the blessing from a natural thinking man, to a spiritually knowledgeable one, a blessing of contentment and enjoyment, and both of these are for evermore. They are eternal.'

'There is a scripture in the Bible saying it all and I will quote it for along with many others I have taken it into myself and I believe with the saying of it over and over, I will be able to live like it says'.

2 Timothy 2; 11

If we died with him we also live with him;

If we endure,

We will also reign with him.

If we disown him,

He will also disown us;

If we are faithless,

He will remain faithful, for he cannot disown himself.'

'This scripture speaks to me daily and I am ever grateful for the Word of God who wrote it through Timothy to be recorded in the Bible'.

'When we go back to the Old Testament, we plainly see what some of the prophets did to receive blessings and we see what some of them did to feel the wrath of God. The important factor in all of what we do, and there is no doubt at all in my heart, it has to be done in obedience'.

'The Ten Commandments are definitely a law for obedience; they are the positive way to live.

I read at the cross on the hill of Calvary, God turned away when his Son took our sins making him dirty as filthy rags this action seems to be extreme, looking at it I can see it is the same when we disobey the commands of the Word, God has to turn away from us if we disobey. He cannot abide sin.

To lose God, for a fraction of time can be quite traumatic, and unless rectified the consequences could be the start of another lesson on obedience'.

'Whether we hear it or not, it is dependent on whether we are committed to God's Holy Spirit and we will hear if we have personally committed to the Words' control.

The Word says 'Blessed rather are those who hear the word of God and obey. *Luke 11:28* and Jesus also said 'my mother and brothers are these who hear the word of God and put it into practice.' ***Luke 8: 21***

'This certainly does not follow when you listen to someone reading the Bible to you.

The person reading it may hear God but you will not if this is how you perceive seeking to hear from Him. There is no blessing and no salvation.

The scripture tells us we ourselves must seek, listen and obey to find any blessing from God'.

'I had many false starts when reading the Bible for I quite blatantly believed I would also hear God if someone read the Bible to me'.

'No one told me this didn't work, it was Brother Moses who put me right, I had to know the Word first who is Jesus, then the realization of the scriptures started to come to life for me'.

As the days passed from negative into a positive way of travelling with Daniel, we can see where the journey has gone.

The same for us as for him it is all new, and Daniel knows each day given to him is for the reason to explore with Godly wisdom the Bible as he is being led into new territory.

Daniel is going to be like everyone who stands straight and tall with God; he is going to be a threat to the beast out there, the beast has no problem at all in whom he uses to try to kill you. To be sure he will not do it himself he likes to manipulate anyone who is uncertain with their own lives into doing the deed for him.

Remember God forbade Satan to destroy Job. The scriptures say this so we can believe, and know in our hearts we also will not be killed.

There are many scriptures on our protection if we believe. An added assurance we have is the fact and truth Jesus shed His blood for us which we are covered with, for we are believers in the Word, believers in Jesus and the cross.

There may be days when we could be caught off guard, when we become less alert and complacent there is a way to avoid this we must stay focused and clothed in the Armour of Christ.

Be alert every day we are given. Each day forward gives us a choice on how we live it, better with faith in the Word than just ambling along believing nothing will touch us, thinking it will only get those out there. Focus on the unseen for it is permanent. ***2 Corinthians 4:17-18*** 'Everyone has a Moses who is just waiting, just waiting to bring them out of their Spiritual Egypt.

Everyone who has the bondage of sins from their past will live as a slave to their bondage. It isn't our timing here, although we may think so, following Moses will happen when we start to hunger and thirst for more from life the moment we feel the pull, of the magnet which will take us away from the dull existence of our daily routine'.

'When we are willing to listen we will hear our name as Samuel did when the Lord called him.'

1 Samuel 3

Understanding the calling will come and with understanding we will know we are being called to follow Christ, and so enter into the Kingdom of Heaven through repentance'.

This calling is through the Word, ***John 1:1-5*** tells us all very clearly *'in the beginning was the Word, and the Word was with God'*

As I said earlier in our travels that means there were two, *'He was with God in the beginning. Through Him all things were made; without Him nothing was made that has been made. In Him was life, and that life was the light of men. The light shines in the darkness, but the darkness has not understood it.*

'I started off this journey dragging you along with me through everything that went with the 'gone by' I am Daniel, and each word written down became the reality of the past and it was coughed up and put to rest in the coffin of sins, through my faith, my belief, and I gave them to God'.

'I saw I was as nothing just a weapon against believing believers, used daily by Satan to either verbally or silently cause dissension wherever I went'.

'It became clear to me as we travelled there is only one way to live, and the instructions for that are found throughout the scriptures, through the eyes of the one who is the Word I was able to see what the Living Lord wanted from me.

'Up till the time I picked up the Bible, I was living on food three times a day, with in betweens when I became hungry, and every day I was hungry for more food seemingly never satisfied with what went into my mouth.

What I was doing was openly rejecting Jesus.

Matthew 21: 42

The stone which the builders tossed aside is now the most important stone of all. This is something the Lord has done, and it is amazing to us.

Although I was unaware of what I was doing for my ignorance was in total innocence.

It would be understandable to ask, how can we know the Word if we are never told where it comes from?

How are we going to know the truth if we do not get enlightenment?

It is Christ who is the light and enlightens all men'. *John 1:9*

How does this come about?

How are we going to understand the Bible if no one tells us we need to know who The Word is?

What is the Bible really about? Is it just another story book to have on a shelf?

As we have travelled, unravelling one enigma of God, we learn we can be in constant communication with Him all the time.

Whenever we want to talk to Him, we only have to open our mouths and he is there. He has promised to never forsake us.

How did that happen?

We have learnt He is the Word; the Word came as man on earth. He was Jesus on earth. Better still he was there at creation.

How do we recognize the Bible is the written 'Word of God', it is not the book which saves us?

The 'Word' saves us.

Do we have to know the Spirit of God?

Yes we do'.

Why are we not taught how to know The Word'?

'The saints of yesteryear listened to the Voice of God through their hearts and believed with such strong faith in everything they did. They believed God was God and he spoke to them'.

'We cannot understand the Bible without knowing who The Word is, and no way will the scriptures mean anything to us if we don't learn this 'who'!

All the scriptures inside the Bible are the records which were taught by the saints, and with Jesus teachings put together into a book for the future growth of mankind?

As I read *__1 John 6:18__* I saw the way for us to understand the Bible and way back when I met Brother Moses my seeking for the real God began.

Brother Moses had the key when he said, we have to know Jesus. What a truthful statement this turned out to be.

It is the Word who said we do not need to have specialized teaching, for we received an anointing the moment we answered our calling, and Jesus who is the Word Himself teaches us everything we need to know in the Spiritual realm'.

'We have already ascertained I was nothing so what made nothing change'?

'It was a hunger and thirst and a need to do what I had so wanted to do in my youth which drove me to change and become who I am now. This was not in one day though, over a period of time'.

'Where had I gone wrong?

Who says I had?'

'I certainly didn't know I was wrong.

How was I to know otherwise if I hadn't been told'?

'Once we learn Christ is the Word of God and the Bible is the records of both Jesus and the prophets all can take shape and fall into the right and proper place.

Our hearts open and receive Jesus, and the outcome is we allow Him to reside within a heart with nothing other than love and gratefulness'. We have said we need both the Old Testament and the New for the Bible tells us so in the scriptures. Moses and all the prophets stated in precise detail what was going to happen to the Lamb of God, and Jesus actually told them after the crucifixion at the tomb, and they were foolish for not believing what had been said about him. *Luke 24:25-27*

'

As it was written from the prophets it shows the scriptures had to be fulfilled to have them as truth.

How did this fulfillment happen?

With the coming of Jesus to the earth, as man?

It states categorically the scriptures must be fulfilled'. *Mark 14: 49*

'The disciples believed on Jesus and why not for they walked with Him and when they saw Jesus after the crucifixion they knew the truth. When Jesus appeared to them this is when they had their understanding opened, for the purpose they might understand the scriptures'. *Luke 24:45.*

'What happened for them has been the same for me' Daniel was explaining to me as we sat writing the last episode of his journey.

It was with excitement I read his last notes and when I had what he wanted put on the screen I started to cry.

Not with anything other than the beauty of this complete transformation of man.

All my life I too had wanted the lost and lonely to be saved and to understand what the Bible was all about, and now with only a few short sentences from a once lost and lonely soul all has been solved?

'Can you hear the Words the angel of the Lord said to Moses from the burning bush'? *Exodus 3:10*

Daniel asked me, and with tears still in my eyes I tried to smile as I said, yes I can.

Daniel continued saying 'you know what is happening don't you?'

Tell me I said.

'I am going to evangelize, and show the people how to become fruitful in a desert situation.

There is a bright light leading me and shining for the glory of the Lord arises upon me.

I know this is not only for me it is for all those who want it, for all those who look up and see for themselves and feel their heart throb and swell with joy for the Lord'. *Isaiah 60:*

'Everyone has to go through the wilderness Moses did, before he was able to do his delivery ministry, Jesus also had a wilderness experience before he preached. John the

Baptist lived in the desert until he was 30 years old. It is this time when we spiritually grow in readiness for the next step in our ordained walk for God.'

'God is going to establish our Spiritual, and bring us together so we can go out and shepherd the sheep.

We must be very careful here for to work with God in the closeness required, we must know we have been called. There must be no jumping the queue, no coming in the back door so to speak'. *John 10: 1-2*

'One thing I do watch and this is going off on goodwill missions, the ones angels would fear to tread'. Daniel said, 'There have been a few times when I made a faux pas and if it hadn't been for God and His mercy I would have been struck down I am sure.

These missions were not in deliberate disobedience to an order you may say, are you sure? For not one of them had been with the leading of the Holy Spirit, so in spiritual reality this makes them out the will of God'.

'They came over the fence, not through the gate as would be proper'.

'While I was travelling through my life with you God was silently working in the background. He was weeding and tidying up all the unnecessary bits and pieces, bringing them into line for the future'.

'I may never know what he was doing, there is one thing I do know though, and it is everyone I meet after this journey will be as he has planned.

For it will be God who brings the people in, he has been preparing them while this book is being written.

We are going to tend a flock of sheep and haul in large nets full of fish as we are shepherds, and fishers of men. We are going to be like Moses tending the flock of Jethro in the desert and where the angel came to him in the burning bush'. ***Exodus 3:1 -2***

'We are going to be fruitful, for we have gone through a desert of events in learning and have come out of it to do the things we so desire.

We have been trained and the skills we have learnt will enable us to stand firm with God as he moves in a mighty way'.

As we listen to Jesus tell us as fishermen to let down the nets we will bring in a haul of millions'.

The journey of Daniel started off as 'I' has ended as 'we' and all of the downs in his life are now gone covered with a mantle of purpose, and this purpose is in the will of God.

I have been the writer, and to put words to paper has been a privilege for in the Spiritual realm The Word is Jesus, and I have been able to bring Him to life for this reading, and write of the unraveling of one enigma.

Daniel needed to become the man God wanted him to be. And when the work was done Daniel would be able to hear the Voice of God, giving him his very own orders to go out and deliver the people just as He did to Moses.

Daniel was looking at me very carefully and I knew he hadn't quite finished he said to me I want you to write this down, I looked for the notes there weren't any, I heard the following words being uttered.

Deuteronomy 8:1-3

Israel, do you want to go into the land the Lord promised your ancestors? Do you want to capture it, live there, and a powerful nation? Then be sure to obey every command I am giving you. Don't forget how the Lord your God has led you through the desert for the past forty years. He wanted to find out if you were truly willing to obey him and depend on him, so he made you go hungry. Then he gave you manna, a kind of food that you and your ancestors had never even heard about. The Lord was teaching you that people need more than food to live- they need every word that the Lord has spoken.

It is the most beautiful scripture to bring to end the journey of Daniel for he was hearing the Voice of God speaking to him as he repeated to me what to write.

I am in no doubt at all Daniel Steppe is going to step out of these pages and follow the command of the Lord from this day forward.

Reality sets in and removes all the chains which have bound us to a world of complete misunderstanding of whom 'The Word' is!

Since becoming a Believing Believer in The Word and following the recorded words of Jesus and the prophets in the Bible has left us in no doubt The Word and the very words in the Bible are taught and believed to be one and the same they both are believed to be a person. The enemy of God can have a field day with you. Never in my hearing have I heard Christians comprehend there is a difference.

The Bible is a book with recorded word.

John 1:1-5 CEV

In the beginning was the one who is called the Word.

The Word was with God and was truly God.

From the beginning the Word was with God.

And with this Word, God created all things.

Nothing was made without the Word.

Everything that was created received its life from him,

And his light gave life to everyone.

The light keeps shining in the dark,

And darkness has never put it out.

Nothing is ever left to chance that can be misconstrued, and we are able to identify who The Word is in the following scripture.

John 1:14 CEV

The Word became a human being and lived here with us.

We saw his true glory,

The glory of the only Son of the Father.

From him all the kindness and all the truth of God

Have come down to us.

The 'Word' became flesh and this 'One' is 'Jesus' the 'Son of God'.

The Word is Jesus; He is a living being within those who have committed themselves to the Spiritual realm they are those who have answered the calling voice of God, and are reborn into the Spirit of God.

The dedicated of those God has chosen and said,

Exodus 3:10

No go to the king! I am sending you to lead my people out of this country.

Amen

WHO ARE YOU

A question we always ask of others.

Never for moment thinking could it be an asking of ourselves.

<u>Who are you?</u>

This is a question for those who have realized to be a child of their creator is what they want to be.

It is for those who do not care about age or status; it is for those who know they need to be a child of God.

And how did this happen.

Could it be the words **'I tell you plainly I never knew you'** were they ringing in your ears, eventually registering to you, leaving you feeling as if a sword had ripped you apart?

Had you heard them before?

What do the words say to you?

Did you get them straight in your face, or did they just creep up on you.

How did you receive them?

By turning away, because you thought they were for someone else, and you never listened?

There are more questions?

Why do you have problems?

Why do you carry them around as if you are proud of them?

Why can't you solve them?

Do you feel the same as everyone else, inconspicuous?

One of a bunch!

What made it impossible for you to have heard those words before?

Why does life seem to be senseless just a waste most of the time?

Is there a key for a better life?

Is the key floating around in limbo above you waiting to be caught, waiting for you to catch a glimpse of it?

Can you see it, and what will you do if you can?

Will the words you heard help you come to terms with where, and who you are?

Does this world belong to an unknown enemy; are you in a fallen world, are you in the enemy's territory?

So many questions being asked every day, and nobody realizes there is but one very simple answer, and without doubt is the absolute truth.

Every Christian, every Believing believer has an enemy!

It is imperative for us to know we must separate God our creator, from Satan our destroyer.

God owns everything on this earth, and nothing ever is done without His okay. He alone can heal and does.

He has flowers, birds, sun, night and day all at His bidding and listen, His love which is for everyone is used as an axis for the world to revolve around.

Even so with such clear and positive words it is vital for us to be aware Satan, is always at hand and ready to contradict God's written Word.

His Written Word is in our Bible, and the first incident of doubt our enemy planted was with Eve.

Genesis 3:1 CEV

'Did God tell you not to eat fruit from any tree in the garden'?

Oh how he loves to cause doubt,

1 Peter 5:8 CEV

'Be on your guard and stay awake. Your enemy, the devil is like a roaring lion, sneaking around to find someone to attack.

Praise God for He has given us the weapons to stand against any of Satan's attacks.

Luke 10:19 CEV

I have given you the power to trample on snakes and scorpions and to defeat the power of your enemy Satan.

Our spiritual knowledge is all based on God's written Word, and clearly shows Believing Believers their living must line up with His Word, if we are to be faithful followers of the one and only God, the creator of all.

So much of our learning is based on circumstances, and we must learn how to deal with these, learning how to handle the most difficult situations bringing us through to the victory of the Cross, and in doing so we allow God to deal with them His way.

This is the only way, and when we consider the outcome of how our natural self would have handled the distressing situations being thrown at us, there had to be a more positive answer.

In life we waste a lot of time planning, getting ourselves deeper into oppression, which is the covering of the devil himself.

God is not the instigator of evil but does allow it to happen for He wants us to lean on Him totally.

Through our own trials which are tried and proven we have learnt the importance of listening to the Holy Spirit who is dwelling within us, and being obedient to every word we hear we know God is telling us He is in control of every situation.

We must invite Him in when He knocks at the door of our heart allowing Him to enter, for He will not come in unless invited, our acceptance is the start of the invitation to Him, it is then, and only then He can and will help us, there is one thing we have to do though we must ask, we must utter words of invitation, we must respond to him.

The strict teaching from the Bible can only be heard if it comes through a vessel totally yielded to God.

Isaiah 30: 21CEV

Whether you turn to the right or to the left you will hear a voice saying, 'this is the road! Now follow it'.

Our human spirit will respond to the spirit of God.

Once we are a child of God and we step back into the flesh, we cause God pain, we can recognize it for the chill of a cold winters' day will run down our spine. Our attitudes do affect God, and through His grace and mercy we get shivers of warning from Him.

This is awesomely frightening when we think of all the wrong words, thoughts or attitudes we have not dealt with from our past, and these sadly make us a target of the enemy's shrinking army.

There is a war going on within us positive against negative.

Two opponents, one who is full of love, gentle and kind the other aggressive and cruel, one is choosing us to destroy the other opponent who is neither pushy nor manipulative and is letting us choose Him.

We must be ever grateful for the revolving love of God and for His Mercy and Grace, not forgetting His forgiving love.

When we repent and ask His forgiveness and forgive ourselves, being clean on the inside we will begin our walk.

Then the words we will hear are the beautiful words spoken at the river Jordan when Christ was baptized by John the Baptist.

As Jesus came up out of the covering of the water a dove hovered above and a voice said, 'This is my Son, whom I love; with him I am well pleased'. Hallelujah!

John the Baptist taught, 'repent for the kingdom of heaven is near.'

To be able to walk daily in the Peace of God, through any adverse situations should truly be the desire of all hearts, and it is very apparent we must live our lives in alignment with

God's written Word, for there is no other way for us to see and feel the Glory of God shining through.

The Shekinah Glory 'the very presence of God'.

It is beautiful in a time of testing to experience the Peace of God, and to know He is being glorified when we sit quietly like Mary did in His soothing presence. **Luke 10:42**

There are many reasons for wanting to read a book, no matter what the reason is, you will read from the Bible sometime for the very purpose of hearing what God is telling you. We must all have a goal.

Your eyes see, and your ears hear and what they hear the heart feeds on and then the mouth can speak words of love and encouragement to other hearts. Once started it goes into automatic control, God's control

The **Holy Spirit** will show you if He wants you to peruse and read it.

The Bible is labeled with your name on it, and this happened the day God conceived you in His heart, the day he gave you a spirit. This was long before you were conceived by your parents.

The Bible says we were given our human spirit our communication to God's Spirit, which comes into being when we say yes to Him.

You were in the womb of your mother when God took the time to tend to you and design the precious being you are. *Psalm 139: 13-18CEV*

Each morning on waking up our thoughts and words are to be positive, we are to believe and know God is with us in our new day.

To know that the **Holy Spirit** is leading is a revelation in itself, you must realize it is your commitment to God that has been the key to the changing things happening to you.

The key you saw floating around in limbo, waiting for you to say '**yes today is the day I am going to open the door to the field of beauty'.**

Your thoughts are starting to be positive they are different, they have been changing, and you are now starting to like who you are. **'Praise the Lord**.'

Asking someone 'Am I different?' will not give you the answer you want; your experience was with your inner self not necessarily visible.

Your actions are not your own, you are compelled to be good all the time, not just when you feel like it, now and again.

You have become a saint who can sin, you are no longer the sinner whose nature is to sin.

Your spirit was born again as soon as you accepted Jesus; this is the reality you are in the light.

Your mind, will, and emotions have not been reborn; they do not have the believer's soul.

If they were born again there would be no reason to have choices.

Your mind will and emotions reside where there is darkness and this is where the unclean spirits stay, along with your physical body suit.

The change is on the inside of you, this is where it has to begin for you will not see the Glory of God unless there is peace within, and this peace surpasses all peace, it is the Peace of God.

You wonder why the animosity you felt for someone or something has suddenly gone.

It has paled to insignificance; you feel a cleansing within you.

The old you, has started to die.

Romans 12:2 CEV

Don't be like the people of this world, but let God change the way you think. Then you will know how to do everything that is good and pleasing to him.

2 Corinthians 5:17 CEV

I *know about one of Christ's followers who was taken up into the third heaven 14 years ago. I don't know if the man was still in his body when it happened, but God certainly does.*

You are beginning to allow God control **of you**.

Please notice it is, 'of you' not 'over you.'

Over you would be likened to the control of the enemy, repeating you would be in **no choice land**.

When you think someone has control over you, there is rebellion, for you like being on your own, doing things your own way, please listen, you have been controlled by the enemy right up to the very moment you said yes to God. Even when you were searching for God, for a better way to live Satan was still your master.

You wanted a new King to reign in your life.

The moment you heard the words denying any knowledge of your being, you stepped forward to enforce the defeat of the enemy.

You undermined the enemy and stopped one of his strategies, his calculated plan to destroy you.

You claimed the Blood and Name of Jesus. Your walk now is with the positive aim to be heard and with your bold declaration of acceptance of the cross and the beyond; you immediately were grafted in as a child of God.

How much better it is, having God looking out for you all day and night as well, for He never slumbers He is ever alert for His Children.

The Bible tells us; God turned His back on His very own Son, **Jesus Christ**, when Jesus took all our sins, diseases, and every other evil thing at the cross.

<u>*Matthew 27: 46 CEV*</u>

'My God, My God why have you forsaken me?'

51, at once the curtain in the temple was torn in two from top to bottom moment the curtain of the temple was torn in two from top to bottom. The earth shook and rocks split apart.

Yes, God turned away.

We believe there can be no dwelling of God where there is sin.

We know the story about Ananias and Sapphira, where they tried to lie to Peter about their stealing in front of the Holy Spirit.

They entered into a no go zone and for this sin they were both struck dead.

<u>*Acts 5: 1-10.CEV*</u>

There is no question about it, God and evil are just not compatible; it is for your good to believe this as soon as possible, go to God, **and stop being a weapon against Him.**

Go to God, go to your Bible, and start to live by it.

There is nothing on this earth which hasn't been created by God, and that includes man manufactured items as well.

The blueprint had to come from somewhere!

The original idea was Gods.

The Bible teaches us God created everything which exists and this means either, spiritually or the materialistic natural things.

<u>*Acts 17:24 CEV*</u>

'This God made the world and everything in it. He is Lord of heaven and earth, and he doesn't need help from anyone.

It tells us again in,

Revelations 4:11 CEV…

You created all things, and by your decision they are and were created.

We all have the breath of God in us, believers and unbelievers.

How do I know that, **The Word** says so when God created Adam [mankind] He breathed in him to give him life?

How does God draw us to Him, we do not suddenly as we are plodding along in our daily routine say, '**today I think I will say 'hi' to Christ and follow Him for a time.'**

Get real.

It is exactly the same as you having this 'Who Are You' book in your hand.

Your name has come up in the Book of Christ for moving house from one camp to the other; you have been drawn here by the breath of God, to be where you are right now.

Hallelujah,

It is time to feel the drawing of Gods breath, the God who created you; it is time to know his breath is a magnet in you.

Our life with or without God is a journey, one which is as long and as hard as you want it to be.

Yes we have the choice of how we live our lives.

In peace and freedom which is with God, or being in a continual up-roar which we get ourselves into by just plodding along on our own ignoring Him, doing what **we** think is best.

Denying Christ, denying the Blood of Jesus, and for whom?

Self! Self! Self!

Nothing ever seems to be quite right; there is always something causing things to go amiss.

It comes down to who we have sitting on the throne. Is it ourselves?

Or do we have Christ on it, in His rightful place?

Why does everyone speak about God in a whisper, as if actually scared of anyone knowing we are in a new place?

Are we ashamed of letting the world know who we are?

Romans 1:16 CEV

'I am proud of the good news! It is God's powerful way of saving all people who have faith, whether they are Jews or Gentiles'

We are new born and have to learn from our Father about this new place, and as we have come as strangers to it we talk quietly.

We have to learn that boldly is the key to receiving the booster injection of confidence.

Being quiet is just what the enemy of God wants us to be, he wants us to fall into deception, believing we do not have demons, the enemy likes to uphold this, we have already said Christian believers can have demons, we have this dark place for them to dwell in.

Suddenly from being Plain Jane, we go through another phase of becoming a world's authority on God, a spirit of religiosity, thus putting people off causing them to hesitate and stop searching and listening.

This is being a stumbling block.

We all know that God created the world we live in, and we all know that God created Adam, and where He was given life,

Genesis 2:7

The Lord formed the man from the dust of the ground and breathed into his nostrils the breath of life and the man became a living being.

Adam had it made in the Garden of Eden the garden of temptation, but as we know there are lessons to learn and the learning comes out of Adams's and Eves' disobedience, to know what the Bible tells us about this incident and all that follows up to the birth of Christ, is there for us to read and hold with inner knowledge. The outcome has us being ever grateful for the Cross.

Are you prepared to risk and take up your,

Responsibility, use your

Initiative, make a

Sacrifice, and use your

Knowledge, to better the world for Christ?

The fall of man is in ***Genesis 3 CEV*** this is the first deception of Satan, hence snakes sliver along the ground, women have pain with child-birth, [our labour], men have to toil the earth so they can eat, [their labour] we have the balance there.

God always balances the events of time.

Disobedience is where deception can really get a hold of you, and the king of it gets his kicks, as long as you are in disobedience you are never going to have the Spirit of God in your hearts.

Are you beginning to understand, why you were not known?

It is common for Christians to be afraid of Satan.

The truth is Satan has no power over you and we have no reason to be afraid of him.

Satan is the king of lies; you can only be Children of God, or children of the Devil. There are no in betweens.

There is no gray matter or a too hard basket as many may have been told to you this is deception trying to make you feel good about yourself.

Listen to what Jesus has said

John 8: 32CEV

'You will know the truth, and the truth will set you free'.

It is very plain is it not?

Hebrews 2:14

Since the children have flesh and blood; he too shared in their humanity so that his death he might destroy him who holds the power of death- that is, the devil. And free those who all their lives were held in slavery by their fear of death.

The next scripture is your booster injection of confidence,

2Timothy 4: 18 CEV

'The Lord will rescue me from every evil attack and will bring me safely to his heavenly kingdom'.

Our strategy is to submit to God and resist the devil, and he will flee from you.

Christians are to be like Jesus and His disciples and not to go out and look for demons to defeat, there will be times when they are in your face and you will have to do so, tell them to be silent and come out… to search for them is not the key you want for the spiritual growth needed to be effective, as an evangelist.

Paul has said it all in

2 Thessalonians 3:3 CEV

But the Lord is faithful and he will strengthen and protect you from the evil one.

If you belong to God you will certainly hear His voice.

The scripture which says this is,

John 10: 27 CEV

"My sheep listen to my voice; I know them and they follow me."

As the **Holy Spirit** continues to leads, and you trust Him there will be no foothold for the devil.

You want to know the Christ, there is a yearning within you, there has begun a hunger that you have never known before, and you do not know where it is coming from, just go with it, for you will not stumble.

And if you do who is going to worry for it is learning in progress, nobody misses out on the lessons of self discipline.

This is what the Lord says.

Jeremiah 31: 9 CEV

They will weep and pray as I bring them home. I will lead them to streams of water. They will walk on a level road and not stumble. I am a father to Israel, my favourite children.

From the birth of Moses there is a story, in **_Exodus 2 CEV_** there was a reason his early life began where it did, in the care of yes, his own mother, in the palaces of Pharaoh, and one could wonder, but all this happened for it was the will of God, part of His plan.

Moses was told to go back to Egypt, for all the men that had wanted to kill him were dead, his very commands came from God, who said ***'bring my people out deliver them for me'***. After a lot of 'ers and ums' I am not good enough, I am not eloquent enough, everything he could think of came forward as an argument, and argue he did.

Moses was given signs by God, the rod he had in his hand turned into a snake, then back to a rod, he had a leprous hand that was made clean as snow, **_Exodus 4 CEV,_** he was so sure that someone else should go in his place. ***Low self esteem, huh?***

He didn't see any easy tasks ahead of him; he saw there would be rebellious Israelites with him.

Remember he grew up as an Egyptian. He knew these people.

One can not help but love Moses, he was a man so normal whatever this is, and he argued with God, lost his cool with the people and didn't do what he was told. Moses whack the rock with the rod, we all do that, we whack Jesus with a rod frequently in our disobedience and so it goes on, but we must also remember that disobedience or not, when Aaron and Miriam spoke against Moses, it was God who called them out and said

***'Listen to My Words*...' _Numbers 12: 6-16 CEV_** tells the story.

Do you know what is being said to you? We must be very careful, of what comes out of our mouths as well as being careful about whom we talk about. There is a little rule you may like to remember.

Watch your words

<u>*Ecclesiastes 5:2. CEV*</u>

Don't talk before you think or make promises to God without thinking them through. God is in heaven and you are on earth, so don't talk too much.

Say nothing about a person unless it passes the triple test!

Is it true? Is it kind? Is it necessary?

If it is true, it may not be kind and necessary.

All three must balance.

We have,

Lord put a seal upon my lips.

Help me to guard with care.

The things I say, and swift repeat.

O, tongue of mine bewares.

It takes a wise person to know what not to say-

And then not to say it.

Moses delivered the Israelites out of Egypt, and through the wilderness where there were troubles enough, with the people arguing and bickering, all blaming yes, Moses.

He was with the Lord all the time like, ***Enoch who walked with the Lord,***

<u>*Genesis 5:24 CEV*</u>

And he stayed doing so whatever went on.

We have water out of the rock, a miracle, there was food from heaven for their good and then we have the plagues of locusts and all the other things sent to them and the bickering still continued.

Our wicks would be getting short, but we must love all, as it says in the Word, **Love others as we love ourselves**. Ouch! And ouch, we do not always see it this way do we?

The miracles of God are limitless, they are countless, God delivered the people through Moses, and they crossed the Jordan to the other side, and there begins another story.

While Moses was bringing Gods people out of Egypt he was given the **Ten Commandants**, ***Exodus 20 CEV*** we also have the 'golden bull', an Asherah pole the people made in rebellion, this did not please Moses, he was a man of God, and the idol certainly was in no way from God.

King Hezekiah of Judah purified the temples when he became king after his father King Ahaz died, destroying the Asherah poles.

Idols made by man to worship.

The story of Hezekiah is found in, ***2Kings, 18-20, 2Chronicles, 29-32, Isaiah 36-39 CEV***

Slowly as you read about the men God chose to work with Him and you get to know them you will start seeing a Real God who is doing the same thing today with His people having a servant deliver His people as He had Moses do from Egypt.

Spiritual Egypt is not a place to be, we should all have a yearning to know God, and to be in the Promised Land with Him.

Why, because we have the breath of God dwelling in us even if we do not actually realize it.

We are to be-

Where He is

Letting Him see us and reside within us so the words of recognition will be the words which fall on our ears.

Who are you meant to be?

Yes a child of God.

Amen

THE WALK OF A
BELIEVING DISCIPLE

The Walk of a Believing Disciple

Galatians 3:1-7 CEV

You stupid Galatians! I told you exactly how Jesus Christ was nailed to the cross. Has someone put an evil spell on you? I want to know only one thing. How were you given God's Spirit? Was it by obeying the Law of Moses or by hearing about Christ and having faith in him? How can you be so stupid? Do you think that by yourself you can complete what God's Spirit started in you?

Have you gone through all of this for nothing? Is it really all for nothing? God gives you his spirit and works miracles in you. But does he do this because you obey the Law of Moses or because you have heard about Christ and have faith in him? The scriptures say that God accepted Abraham because Abraham had faith. And so, you should understand that everyone who has faith is a child of Abraham.

<u>The Walk of a Believing Disciple</u>

Being a Saved Believing does not necessarily mean you are walking as one.

Being a Believing disciple **does not necessarily** mean you are following Jesus.

The crowd has many comments about another's walk, some complementary some derogatory, and you will find the comments come from those who are not a Believing disciple of the True God.

Jesus was a teacher on earth for three years, have we ever remembered, he was actually on the earth for thirty three years, and in that time he was abused with words, treated as if nothing, then murdered, **and for what**?

What was his crime?

Did He commit one?

No!

It was us, and we are still committing the sins Jesus was crucified for.

The worldly have become so selfish and their only thought is about self.

Anything done to another in selfish intent cannot have the Love of God in it; if man persecutes a **Believing, a Believing Believer** today his intent is the same as the Roman soldiers who killed Jesus at the Cross.

They are like Barrabbas. Do you know who he is?

Mark 15:9-13 CEV

Pilate asked them, do you want me to free the king of the Jews? Pilate knew that the chief priests had brought Jesus to him because they were jealous. But the chief priests told the crowd to ask Pilate to free Barabbas. Then Pilate asked the crowd, 'what do you want me to do with this man you say is the king of the Jews?' They yelled 'Nail him to the cross'.

Jesus was persecuted and betrayed.

Just as dedicated Believing Believers are for no other reason than they emulate Jesus.

Once again with every criticism Jesus is taken to the cross; they are murdering a **Believing Disciple**.

What is the follower of Jesus,' real crime?

Is it because they are not listening to you, or following and obeying you? Not doing things your way?

Jesus was the most devoted **Disciple** of all time and as the years move on, He will still be taught, He will always be a **Disciple**, a follower of His Father in Heaven. He will always be followed for the Believing Believers will see He is.

Jesus did nothing unless His Father in heaven told Him to.

Yes, there are teachers who follow the Word of the Bible, and there are preachers who do the same, are they to be persecuted as well?

Do you want a church built by man, or one built by God?

Where did Jesus teach? Was it in a temple built by man?

No, it was beside a lake, beside a well, and on a hillside where the multitudes gathered.

It was where He was.

Did he not display a rage at selling in the temple?

And what are we being taught today?

The things which are abominations to God are entering into what is meant to be a Holy place?

Man has allowed this.

Believing Believers fortunately do not accept the rules of man on the Spiritual level; they feel unclean being in the presence of an abomination of God.

God overcame this difficulty by giving to His Believing Disciples Divine access to Him.

There doesn't have to be a building made from bricks and mortar.

Believing Believers are the temples of God; they are vessels who have the indwelling of the Holy Spirit through their commitment to Christ Jesus, as they walk and breathe they have the living God residing within their heart, and the Bible will confirm this.

Believing Believers have **deliberately** chosen to answer the Divine calling on their lives, and these same devoted disciples view their life through the eyes of Jesus not man, so yes, there will be disagreement with their way of living.

Those who enter into manmade buildings, with their man ideas believing they are right will lie to the man of God, the preacher or teacher from the pulpit, they will say what a lovely word or sermon, then go out and curse it.

Why did Jesus bother we ask ourselves?

How great is His love for us?

It is our love for Him; which He ignited with His own love into a consuming fire to share with other kindred spirits?

Why can you not show your love to **Believing Believers**?

It is He, Jesus Christ whom they follow**.**

It is He who is Our Saviour, they are victorious vessels through his crucifixion, for the Christ our Saviour saved us from those who are trying to have us follow them, and do what they say we should do!

They demand us to live their way of life!

This demand takes away choice.

Why would a **Believing Believer** throw away a life of peace for a life of strife? Can the truth not be seen?

Believing Believers are not asking you to follow them personally; they are leading you to follow Jesus.

It was Jesus, who saved us. People are unable to save anyone, or anything, they can only lead and show the gateway to heaven. If Jesus wants to bring someone to Him, He will have prepared the way first.

There are fifteen rules to being a dedicated Believing Believer, and they must be followed. For our discipleship depends upon this.

The way we walk and talk must be Godly if we want to claim the title, with truth. **'I am a Believing Disciple'.**

Many walk, and don't talk, as many talk, and do not walk.

Defining the word disciple = follower.

If you are following a recipe of a cookery author it doesn't matter what your cooking is like, you follow in **Blind Acceptance** the authors' instructions, and you believe the recipe will be a success.

It is the same in anything we do; we are following a set of rules written for instruction. The first set of rules followed, came from our parents and they were followed with blind acceptance, and shared with others the ups and downs of these rules.

Being a disciple is all about acceptance and sharing.

Defining the word follower = hanger-on, devotee, fan, admirer, disciple.

These are very simple words with nothing outrageous or threatening in them, unless they are taken out of concept and used for ulterior motives such as **making someone follow a false belief**.

A belief which has nothing to confirm it as being righteous or positive.

Being a **Believing Believer** there has to be a separation, a setting apart from the worldly; and it may seem your detachment will look like 'being led astray'.

Yes you are moving into a new realm, you have seen the two paths side by side one is Godly, and the other is not.

It is lack of understanding which brings about conflict, especially within families on **Believing Discipleship**.

Christ has become the one whom you have chosen to follow, He has called you and you have chosen to become dedicated to a walk, only **Believing Believers** follow.

It was not you calling Him, you were called by Him, and you listened, and then obeyed.

The first thing when growing in the walk of a committed **Believing Believer** will be from within oneself. The peace you now feel for the first time in year's makes you want to share with everyone all you know, about God. Those against God will feel their hostile spirits rising within thus causing them to be belligerent, this is only through their lack of understanding and yes, they will rise against you.

It has already happened with the false being thrown out of heaven. ***Revelations 12:7 CEV*** We do not have to go there again.

A **Believing Believer** follows the doctrine of another and spreads it by teaching, or preaching the Good News of none other than Jesus Christ.

When there are hidden issues unattended from our past or present, those opposing the **Believing Believer** will look for another to blame for the attitudes they carry.

It is ironical for they will always blame the messenger.

Jesus was a carpenter, so initially he would have been a Believer of his teacher Joseph, he learnt the basics then followed his own Fathers plans, and built from them.

Any builder will tell you there has to be a foundation to build upon; the roof cannot go on a building first.

Believing Believers is a means of which Believers grow in the Lord Jesus Christ, and their blind acceptance will be equipped by the Holy Spirit.

The Holy Spirit resides within a Believers heart and in this way they are able to overcome the pressures and trials of their daily living, learning to be a Believing Believer shows those who are chosen to see a light within, and will also want to live a life emulating the Christ Jesus.

The Bible is not a book for Believers to use as a weapon against another; it is a book of instructions for the **Believing Believer** to live by.

Those who oppose **Believing Believers** are basically against Jesus Christ.

They haven't picked up their cross!

For those who are **Believing Believers** do not be discouraged, for the Lord is ever watching and the choice being made was your choice, the chosen walk and life you want to live. Opposition, ridicule, cruelty from others will happen for following the Christ, we too will suffer for yes, these things all happened to Him.

Believing **Believers** = dedicated to the following of the one who gave his life for us.

Believing **Believers**= have committed their own life to Jesus and will not be swayed to live any other way.

Believing Believers = **follow Jesus,** they share **His Word, they believe in Jesus**

The Ten Commandments are God's law, and discipline for Believing Believers.

Exodus 20 1: 17 CEV

God said to the people of Israel:

'I am the Lord your God, who brought you out of Egypt, where you were.

Do not worship any god except me.

Do not make idols that look like anything in the sky or on earth or in ocean under the earth. Don't bow down and worship idols. I am the Lord your God, and I demand all your love. If you reject me, I will punish your families for three or four generations. But if you love me and obey my laws, I will be kind to your families for thousands of generations. Do not misuse my name. I am the Lord your God, and I will punish anyone who misuses my name. Remember that the Sabbath Day belongs to me. You have six days when you can do your work, but the seventh day of each week belongs to me, your God. No one is to work on that day- not you, your children, your slaves, your animals, or the foreigners who live in your towns. In six days I made the sky, the earth, the oceans, and everything in them, but on the seventh day I rested. That's why I made the Sabbath day a special day that belongs to me.

Respect your father and your mother, and you will live a long time in the land I am giving to you. Do not murder.

Be faithful in marriage.

Do not steal.

Do not tell lies about others.

Do not want anything that belongs to someone else. Don't want anyone's house, wife or husband, slaves, bullocks, donkeys or anything else.

The last five rules are based on the Ten you have just read.

11. Jesus is to be first in all things.

Mark 8: 34-38 CEV

Jesus then told the crowd and the disciples to come closer, and he said.

If any of you want to be my followers, you must forget about yourself.

You must take up your cross and follow me. If you want to save your life, you will destroy it.

But if you give up your life for me and for the good news, you will save it. What will you gain, if you own the whole world but destroy yourself?
What could you give to get back your soul? Don't be ashamed of me and my message among these unfaithful and sinful people! If you are the Son of Man will be ashamed of you and when he comes in the glory of his Father with the holy angels.

The Christian Disciple is to be set apart from the world, their focus should always be on the Lord and they should always want to be pleasing Him, this is **in every area of their lives.** Self-centeredness must go and the clothing of Christ Centeredness is to be worn.

12. **The teachings of Christ are to be followed;**

John 8:31-32 CEV
Jesus told the people who had faith in him, if you keep on obeying what I have said, you are truly my disciples.
You will know the truth, and the truth will set you free.

It is not enough knowing the Word, we must be obedient to it as well, and obedience is the test of our faith in God. Our example is the perfect obedience of Jesus when he lived on earth; this was right up to the very end of His life.

13. Fruitfulness

John 15: 5-8 CEV
'I am the vine; and you are the branches.

If you stay joined to me, and I stay joined to you then you will produce lots of fruit. But you can't do anything without me. If you don't stay joined to me, you will be thrown away. You will be like dry branches that are gathered up and burnt in a fire.

Stay joined to me and let my teachings become part of you. Then you can pray for whatever you want, and your prayer will be answered. When you become fruitful disciples of mine, my Father will be honoured.

Believers are to remain abiding in Christ this is their work, and by doing so the Holy Spirit will produce the fruit.

The fruit produced is the results of obedience.

With the walk of continued obedience, behavior will change.

The place of change will be in hearts, and it is from our hearts, thoughts, words, and actions will change this happened only through the power of the Holy Spirit, and as others see the difference in a Believing Believer they will want to know why. **We can not change on our own.**

14. We will love other disciples

John 13: 34-35 CEV

'But I am giving you a new command. You must love each other, just as I have loved you. If you love each other, everyone will know that you are my disciples.

The evidence of our being a member of God's own family is seen in how other Believers show their love to you.

1John 3: 10 CEV

This is how we know who the children of God are and who the children of the devil are: Anyone who does not do what is right is not a child of God; nor is anyone who does not love his brother.

1 Corinthians 13:1-13 CEV

What if I speak all languages of humans and angels? If I did not love others, I would be nothing more than a noisy gong or a clanging cymbal.

What if I could prophesy and understand all secrets and all knowledge?

And what if I had faith that moved mountains?

I would be nothing, unless I loved others.

What if I gave away all that I owned and let myself be burnt alive?

I would gain nothing, unless I loved others.

Love is kind and patient, never jealous, boastful, proud, or rude.

Love isn't selfish or quick tempered.

It doesn't keep a record of wrong that others do.

Love rejoices in the truth, but not evil.

Love is always supportive, loyal, hopeful and trusting.

Love never fails!

Everyone who prophesies will stop, and unknown languages will no longer be spoken.

All that we know will be forgotten.

We don't know everything, and our prophecies are not complete.

But what is perfect will someday appear,

And what isn't perfect will disappear.

When we were children,

We thought and reasoned as children do. But when we grew up, we quit our childish ways.

Now all we can see of God is like a cloudy picture in a mirror.

Later we will see him face to face.

We don't know everything, but then we will, just as God completely understands us.

For now there are faith, hope, and love.

But of these three, the greatest is love.

Philippians 2: 3-5 CEV

Don't be jealous or proud, but be humble and consider others more important than yourselves.

Care about them as much as you care about yourselves and think the same way that Christ Jesus thought:

It is plain to see we are to think more highly of others than ourselves,

Our attitude should be the same as Jesus Christ's.

Believing Believers example is from the perfection of Jesus Christ.

15. Evangelism = making Believers of others.

It is sharing our faith and telling <u>non-believers</u> about the changes in our lives which will do that.

Whether we are a beginner, in the knowledge of Jesus or not we are to share with those who do not know.

Matthew 28: 18 -20 CEV

Then Jesus came to them and said, 'I have been given all authority in heaven and on earth.

Go to the people of all nations and make them my disciples. Baptize them in the name of the Father, the Son, and the Holy Spirit, and teach them to do everything I have told you. I will be with you always, even until the end of the world.

What can be better than to know that Jesus is with us now, and will be until the end of the age?

Would you want to throw this away and follow someone who has no knowledge what real living is?

No **Believing Believer** will ever do so; they will love and welcome another to come under the protection they receive, all day and all night every day and every night, it makes no matter your age, your status in the world, or your creed, God loves you, and Jesus died for you.

Believing Believers are waiting for you to make the choice, to listen to the voice of God.

Matthew 22:14 CEV

Many are invited, but only a few are chosen.

Pick up your cross and walk the walk of faith, it is by faith a **Believing Believer** is able to live out their life without stress.

Forgiveness has been asked for, and received.

They know whatever they seek can only be received by no other means than by their faith.

Don't be mistaken in thinking it is by works you will get to heaven, it is certainly not the way.

God has shown us in the Bible, when following the rules of man we will get nowhere.

The Bible says no one is justified by the law of man, in the sight of God.

<u>Galatians 3:11CEV</u>

No one can please God by obeying the Law. The scriptures also say, 'the people God accepts because of their faith will live.

Jesus was rejected by the Pharisees, as many Believing Believers are and why, for speaking only the truth; they speak out about the worthlessness of righteous deeds, telling people it is only faith in Jesus Himself which will save them?

It is obvious there is **only one** way to go, and this is the way of the Lord.

It is through faithful dedication and commitment in the knowing of Jesus, and allowing the Holy Spirit to personally equip you for eternity, which keeps us a dedicated **Believing Believer**.

THE LOVE OF JESUS CHRIST

Holds all His Authority

By Val Taylor

The Love of Jesus Christ

Holds all Authority

For without it there is no authority

A dedicated Believing Believer will do everything in **love,** and this **love** is the unfettered **love** of the Christ, who's Spirit, is dwelling within their heart.

The authority the **love** of Jesus gives to the Believer is beyond our comprehension.

Authority of the work portrayal was given to the Believing Believer by Jesus and we follow it in **His love**.

Matthew 28: 18.Cev

Then Jesus came to them and said, 'All authority in heaven and on earth! Go to the people of all nations and make them my disciples. Baptize them in the name of the Father, the Son, and the Holy Spirit, and teach them everything I have told you. I will be with you always, even until the end of the World.

This authority has drawbacks, for within the commands are hidden obligations which are to be followed in total obedience.

Misunderstandings have touched many in the world, for the command is to baptize and teach what we have learned ourselves from Jesus, and those we reach for, are the 'non believers'.

Believers in Jesus Christ have already found Him, and have dedicated and committed their life to following the Christ; other Believing believers are of no concern to them for they are already saved.

The unreliability of our own love does not deliver to the unbeliever a message for the most times without prejudice.

The love of the world is too flighty, too easily swayed by the devil.

You may not like to read the following it is reality though if you are not for Jesus you will be for the devil.

The Worldly are children of the devil.

They are non believers of Jesus,

Before we were born earthly beings, at our conception God gave us a spirit, and it is this very spirit which answers the call of God in our lives.

We answer the call of God and we ask forgiveness of our past sins and this is when we receive the Love of Jesus through His Spirit, the Holy Spirit. And we become a saved soul.

We need the Love of Jesus and His Spirit, because human love alone is inadequate for the work of God.

It can be moody, disruptive and at its worse destructive.

It lies and cheats to get its own way.

The Spirit of God, within us shows a way out of bondage, and through our love for God we are able to move into following Him.

With the realization it is the very love of God; His never-ending love which satisfies the heart of mankind and by His guiding forward, we will be compelled into seeking more of Jesus.

As God only wants wellbeing for His created ones there can only be true happiness by loving Him, a good reason for our creation is to give pleasure to the God of Love through our own love.

God wants our love; and through our love of God we have been given a visible world, a world with form.

From birth we had to learn how to love.

The most important action in love is eye contact.

When a mother looks straight in the eyes of her new born child she has started the bonding of human love.

No matter the child can not focus, it will feel this love.

Our parents are our first love example.

There are circumstances where this does not happen and sad to say this is where a child is deprived of the first love bonding, and the learning is hindered, as the child grows learning how to focus and what is seen will either show love or a life searching for it.

Believers always deliver a message from the heart, always with the unblemished love of Christ.

Our own love has self conditions; when we get what we want we will love the giver for a time; this love does not come from the heart, for most times it comes from our mind, our feelings or our emotions.

To have the love of Jesus within means we can lean on it, and the combination of this love blend covers all the prejudices.

The love of the giver of his blood and name sets us free.

We say we would love to be this or that; our loving does not actually make it happen.

We would love a slim line car, we would love a new house, and this love is motivated by our wanting what our eyes, we see our wanting.

It is not from the heart.

Do we need a slim line car? Etc!

Pure love of God has the exceptional attributes of such profound purpose it can only come from the Divine, the Deity of a Spiritual being.

Pure love can be characterized as being Jesus Christ.

The God who created us had a purpose for His chosen people, and those chosen will be filled with the Love of Jesus.

Defining, A Believing Believer = someone who believes <u>IN</u> Jesus Christ and <u>ON</u> His word

Defining, a Believer = someone who believes there is a Jesus Christ, but has not dedicated their lives to Him.

Romans 8: 28-30 CEV

We know that God is always at work for the good of everyone who loves him. They are the ones God has chosen for His purpose, and he has always known who his chosen ones would be. He had decided to let them become like his own Son, so that his Son would be the first of many children. God then accepted the people he had already decided to choose and he has shared his glory with them.

Ephesians 1: 11-12 CEV

God always does what he plans, and that's why he appointed Christ to choose us. He did this so that we Jews would bring honour to him and be the first ones to have hope because of him.

1 Peter 2: 7-8 CEV

You are followers of the Lord, and that stone is precious to you. But it isn't precious to those who refuse to follow him. They are the builders who tossed aside the stone that turned out to be the most important one of all. They disobeyed the message and stumbled and fell over the stone, because they were doomed.

Jesus Christ established **His Church, His Believers**, to train future Believers for God's Kingdom so they could share in teaching salvation to the multitudes; he knew these Believing Believers would be needed to teach others with the love He Himself taught with.

The chosen would then impart this love to unbelievers to show them what the life of Christ was, and is.

Remember the choice of where anyone wants to be only belongs to them, and when speaking to an unbeliever with the Holy Spirit's leading, the Lord will have already begun pulling in the net.

We are fishers of men!

This peaceful existent does not exclude trials and tribulations for we are living in the world naturally, and Believing Believers live, with God's Spirit in the world yes spiritually apart from it.

Seemingly contradictory but true.

The command to go out and be fishers of men is again mistaken to mean, go to the believing believers of Jesus.

To be with Believing Believers is to be in the company of the Lord, and so in this company we should be at peace, this does not always follow.

Unbelievers do not argue with God for they do not know Him, they do not want to compete, and they do not hold any false attitudes.

The Believing Believer rattles more cages than anyone known, to be walking with Jesus and knowing His very own love can be like 'waving a red rag to a raging bull'.

The believing Believer interprets the Bible with the Love of Jesus, and in the exact way Jesus desires His Word to be delivered.

Believing Believers have the Spirit of Jesus dwelling within their hearts, they know and do everything through it.

The love of Jesus will have His Believers thinking of a goal, and this goal will be an unbeliever, the love of Jesus will help keep this goal in the Believer's sight, they will see and call on their goal with love, and like Jesus did, they will suffer for the goal, bringing it into a place of exaltation.

Exaltation is the aim the Believing Believer leads a un- believer toward.

The Believing Believer doesn't have to do very much they just have to be ready, and be there when called.

This could be five times in a day or once in a year, it is not relevant when, it is relevant where.

It is in this exalted place the love of Jesus will let the unbeliever see the fruit of their new thinking, they will see their calling, they will see the suffering of their past, and the love Jesus freely gives to the nonbeliever will envelope them with a feeling of the delicious warmth of happiness, and their very own exaltation, it is then their own harvest can be reaped.

It is the believing Believer who with the Love of Jesus walks into the territory of an unbeliever and displays a love, which cannot be rejected.

It is portrayed gently with caring, and with the loving insight of what the unbeliever is going through in the world of man.

Another misunderstanding is; Believing Believers must never be firm and harsh!

How can you learn if you are not rebuked?

Does a mistake carry on being a mistake?

Yes it does unless; a follower of Jesus speaks the truth!

John 17:17 CEV

Your word is the truth. So let this truth be completely yours.

Jesus is love! And He taught everything with love.

The love of Jesus is totally misunderstood, the understanding out there is one should never speak harshly, one should never correct another, and to live the 'Jesus' way which is to take everything on the chin and tolerate it.

This is absolute rubbish. Jesus didn't! He walked away from the grumblers, who wanted to throw Him over the cliff, a death before the time. He ripped into the Pharisees with a tongue of loud rebuke many times.

If you are ignoring wrongdoings you do not love, for love is seeing that everyone around you is receiving, the very best all the time and the correct and only way is, **the way of Jesus.**

You as a Believing Believer determined = firmly decided, to save lives to stop anything from hindering the truth of Jesus, will step in the gap of anything or anyone who wants to stop the love of Jesus being seen.

Believers are to go through adversity with their brothers.

They will stand in front of them to save their lives, they will love them and take the bullet if need be, without question.

This is the truth and it shows the love of Jesus.

Jesus did not tolerate hypocrites, or falseness of any kind, and neither should a Believing Believer.

If there is misunderstanding of the Believing Believer, and they are spoken ill about, they know not be offended for as the Bible says Jesus was hated first. And any hatred directed at you has been dealt with at the cross. It is only there for the enemy of God is trying to intimidate you.

Matthew 10: 34-36 CEV

Don't think that I came to bring peace to the earth! I came to bring trouble, not peace. I came to turn sons against their fathers, daughters against their mothers, and daughter-in-laws against their mother-in-laws. Your worst enemies will be in your own family.

Jesus is saying very plainly it is ones own family which will turn against a Believing Believer. It is plain enough families will not understand followers of Jesus for a Believer's speaking will be out of their love for Jesus, not the worldly love the non- dedicated knows. The non- dedicated do not carry the 'Spirit of Christ', they only believe in Him. Meaning they do not walk on His very Words. They walk on the words which suit them.

Jesus prefers the battle rather than the 'best pal' syndrome, for it is a battle which saves a spiritual life; not the best pal cuddly friends saga.

His rebuke in the next scripture is severe and bitter.

Matthew 11: 21-24 CEV

You people of Chorazin are in for trouble.

You people of Bethsaida are in for trouble too!

If the miracles that took place in your towns had happened in Tyre and Sidon, the people there would have turned to God long ago. They would have dressed in sackcloth and put ashes on their heads. I tell you that on the Day of Judgment the people of Tyre and Sidon will get off easier than you will.

The people of Capernaum, do you think you will be honoured in heaven? You will go down to hell!

If the miracles that took place in your place had happened in Sodom, that town would still be standing. So I tell you on the Day of Judgment the people of Sodom will get off easier than you.

Matthew 12: 33-39 CEV

Jesus rebuked those who were Pharisees, and he didn't hesitate in calling them names, he called them evil, vipers and adulterous, the Scribes He called hypocrites for they were teaching wrong doctrines.

Today wrong doctrine is still being taught; yes this teaching is still happening.

Matthew 15: 12, and Matthew 16: 4 CEV

Tells us the Pharisees were offended at these harsh words, and it is the same today when the Loving Truth of the Word of God is spoken to Pharisees. It seems impossible for them to hear the Word or to see the truth the reason is their ears and eyes are closed.

They are still out there, just because the years have passed by since Jesus the man, was on Earth it has not changed the fact Pharisees were there, as they are today.

So, when a Believing Believers speak harsh correction to you, and as they carry the Christ within their hearts they will be speaking the absolute truth of Jesus, in His divine love and authority.

Matthew 16: 6-11CEV

Jesus then warned them, 'Watch out! Guard against the yeast of the Pharisees and Sadducees.

As Believing Believers this is what we should do?

As Believing Believers, as 'Jesus followers' is the love of Jesus not within us; do we not have the same love He spoke with when He spoke out about the warnings on false doctrine?

Our love is no less when we speak out giving the same warnings?

The following scripture has such impact and many Believing Believers have cringed when they realized they are doing what Peter was rebuked about, speaking what is **NOT OF GOD**. Believing Believers should only allow Godliness out of their mouths, they should be very careful of what they utter.

Matthew 16: 22-23 CEV

Peter took Jesus aside and told him to stop talking like that. He said 'God would never let this happen to you, Lord!'

Jesus turned to Peter and said, 'Satan, get away from me! You're in my way because you think like everyone else, and not like God.'

Jesus corrected his friend so he could turn, and follow the right and correct path. He rebuked Peter for his ignorance, and He did it in love.

Matthew 21: 12-13.CEV

Jesus once more showed the Love of God when he threw the money changers out of the temple; a temple was and is not to be a place of business.

It is not correct to make profit from those who come to worship God.

God provides all the money ever needed in our lives.

He is the provider of all our needs.

Remember the word says 'Temples of God are the people'.

When a temple is making money out of God, we will see exactly how many types of temples there really are!

When there is mixing with those temples who use God for their own means, there will also be 'blind guides' and 'fools', with no righteousness or good being seen.

We cannot do evil if God is within us, for evil and God do not mix. **Ever! Ever! Ever!**

We do not understand the Love of God unless we have the Holy Spirit within us, and if He is, a light will be seen.

The Love of Jesus was available the moment Jesus was accepted as the Saviour.

A Child of God was grafted into the family, the dedication of life learning, and through the Love of Jesus, leading a Believer into a dedicated Believing Believer.

It was at this time the truth was learnt about rebuking and renouncing, for to rebuke we do so sharply, and to renounce we reject or disown.

Both of these Jesus did, and so must the Believing Believer for the correction must be what God did Himself through his very own love within us.

Jesus was certainly not too bothered if He hurt feelings, to correct there has to be rebuking and renouncing, and this is the walk Believing Believers have chosen to take.

Jesus did all for the very reason He had love for each one of us, He warned.

Heed it is as the Word says; only those He loved he rebuked.

Hebrews 12: 5-12 CEV

None of you have yet been hurt in your battle against sin.

But you have forgotten that the scriptures say to God's children,

When the Lord punishes you, don't make light of it, and when he corrects you, don't be discouraged.

The Lord corrects the people he loves and disciplines those he calls his own.

Be patient when you are being corrected!

This is how God treats his children. Don't all parents correct their children? God corrects all his children, and if he doesn't correct you, then you don't really belong to him. Our earthly fathers correct us, and we still respect them. Isn't it better to be given true life by letting our Spiritual Father correct us?

Our human fathers correct us for a short time, and they do it as they think best. But God corrects us for our own good, because he wants us to be holy, as he is. It is never fun to be corrected. In fact, at the time it is always painful. But if we learn to obey by being corrected, we will do right and live in peace.

Now stand up straight! Stop your knees from shaking, and walk a straight path.

There are times in a Believing Believers life he hears someone speaking not in the truth of God.

We are to listen to God, and not to worldly Believers who believe in themselves, and wish to profit from their own Words.

The truth is, there are those who hold positions who believe they are speaking for God, if they were hearing why are they not bringing in saved Believing Believers, all willing to be trained and go out as dedicated Believing Believers, are there two standards a false one, as well as a true one who delivers through His Love the Truth of Jesus,.

Be very sure the God you teach is the Real God of the Bible.

Be sure not to be afraid of mankind, and teach the True God.

The God of the Bible did rebuke harshly, and He destroyed those who disobeyed Him. He even destroyed complete nations.

Romans 1: 16 CEV

I am proud of the good news! It is God's way powerful way of saving all people who have faith, whether they are Jews or Gentiles.

God sends out Believing Believers to be messengers He works through them, and they are those whom He knows and loves.

He has them looking for a goal to bring closer to Him, and the ultimate is this goal will become a dedicated Believing Believer who will learn and bring in another goal, and so it goes on.

Another and another is caught and brought in to be a Believing Believer in the very army of teachers displaying,

The Love of Jesus holds all Authority

Amen